EYES, E͟

&

TREACHEROUS

MINDS

BY

Chris Breddy

DEDICATION

*This book is dedicated to all the men and women
who secretly keep the country as safe as they can.*

ACKNOWLEDGMENTS

I'd like to thank my publishing team for steering me through the fog and getting my book published. To my tolerant wife Karen, who, whilst I tapped away at the computer, supplied endless cups of coffee and thought I was studying Morse code. Finally, to my friends; those who supplied advice and others who unknowingly created characters in the book.

CONTENTS

1

They heard four words. Four words that sent shivers down certain peoples' spines. And four words that had to be kept secret. Those words were flashed south to an office by the Thames. And although the words 'kill the Prime Minister' were never taken lightly, the majority of the people in the UK were in agreement. Get rid.

"It seems," began the authoritative voice of Adrian, "that a new terrorist cell may be planning something nasty on the mainland and our friends at Cheltenham are, at this moment, trying to trace the call."

The small group of people sitting around the table shook their heads, acknowledging the significance of their boss's concern. Nothing had been heard from those friends across the pond. Nothing had flagged up any warnings. Nothing had been so serious. And nothing had happened in the UK for quite some time.

Until that morning.

"All we can hope," Adrian continued, "is that the caller, said to be a woman with a lilting Irish accent, might make another careless phone call. But until that happens, you three will have to keep your ears open."

Fiona, Greg, and Jack looked at each other, wondering when that might happen. Experience told them it usually did. One careless phone-call usually led to another.

And several days later the second mistake was made.

2

GCHQ had pinned the call down to be somewhere around Holborn, and that chunk of London was where thousands of people lived.

Adrian looked at Jack and his team and tapped his pencil on the top of the table.

"Reckon it's time to start work."

Another phone call had been picked up at Cheltenham and the voice was a match. The woman had been careless again, only this time she'd stayed on the line long enough for the number to be traced. Jack said it'd happen. He wasn't always right, but this time he was. It was time to leave the office.

Having checked through her address list, Fiona was the first to find it, but she told Jack later that extra hands would be needed. Although the building had three storeys, it only had one entrance into it from the street, and that was secured by a numerically coded lock, adding that the rear entrance also had just the one door. And it too was secured by a similar device.

Finding the owner of the property didn't pose a problem. It just took a quick and friendly call 'from the council' as she put it, regarding the payment of council tax.

Minutes later and Fiona learnt that the building contained eight flats. From that piece of information, she was told that only two of the flats were occupied by women and the one that was occupied by an Irish woman was the only flat in the entire block with a landline.

It was then, after Jack had told Fiona and Greg about other plans that were being put in place, that he asked Fiona to make another phone call.

3

It was on Wednesday morning, that a dark haired twenty-six-year-old Briony McCormack left Charing Cross tube station feeling on top of the world. Two things were making her feel happy. The first of those was that the sun was shining and that cheered her up because it'd been raining for the last week and she was totally fed up with it. The second thing that was making her feel good was that she was taking on an assistant.

She needed one, because, whenever she went out, she had to put the closed sign on the door and that wasn't good for business. Her boss simply told her to put an ad in the shop window and when a bloke from one of the London Borough's job centres saw it on his way to work, he rang the shop to ask if they could send someone over for the job.

Naturally she jumped at the offer.

And walking along the Strand to Trafalgar Square Briony wondered what the new person would be like, hoping for someone who wouldn't be too troublesome. She'd learnt from experience that they could be.

As she rounded the corner into Whitehall, she saw who she guessed was her new assistant standing next to the door of the small souvenir gift-shop that she ran.

Leaning against the separating wall between the shop and its neighbour, a young woman was standing with one foot on the pavement and the other flat against the wall behind her. She was reading *The Sun* and as Briony got closer she could see that this was the new assistant. She was wearing a torn mock-leather bomber-jacket, a thin black t-shirt, torn jeans, and trainers that looked like they wouldn't get through the day. It was also obvious to Briony that this woman was short of cash.

"Hello," she said in her pleasant Irish accent when she unlocked the door to the shop. "I bet you're Bev, aren't you?"

The woman nodded but didn't smile.

Hope this isn't going to be difficult, Briony thought as she opened the door.

"Come on in then, let's get you started."

Following her into the shop Bev tucked the newspaper under her arm and handed the crumpled A4 envelope to her.

"The job centre told me t'give you this," she grunted shyly, looking down at the floor, not wanting to make eye contact. Her voice sounded hard and monotonous – that made Briony hope it might come to life as the day went on.

"Well, before we do anything else," she said to Bev as she took the envelope, "let's get the kettle on then I'll show you round."

Bev walked behind Briony into the back room where a small kitchenette and loo were.

"Coffee?" she asked as she switched the kettle on.

Head down and looking embarrassed, Bev nodded and muttered thanks.

"Milk? Sugar?"

Another nod, then what sounded like 'please' escaped from Bev's lips.

By the time they'd finished their coffee Briony had read through the two and a half pages of information about her new assistant, knowing then, that she'd have to keep an eye on her.

The job centre's documents told Briony that Bev had not long been released from a two-year stretch in prison. And the charges of carrying a weapon, assault, and handling stolen goods were all but a few of the offences.

4

"Er, hello, is Mrs Bromley there at all?"

It was an elderly lady from the landlord's office.

"Sorry but I think you've got the wrong number," a young woman replied.

"Oh, I'm er terribly sorry, m'love. I'm new here and I thought that was your name. Got to get m'records up to date, so can I ask you your name and your flat number?"

She sounded totally confused.

"At this rate I'll never get them finished."

The younger woman began laughing. Friendly like.

"I'm Miss McCormack. Briony. And I'm in flat number five."

"What a lovely name that is. And is Briony spelt with an E?"

The woman told her it wasn't but still spelt it out for her.

"Thank you Miss McCormack m'dear," she continued as she noisily shuffled papers about on her desk. "If only the others there were as nice as you. Thank you."

"Oh think nothing of it," the other woman insisted.

"Oh! Yes," the elderly lady began once more. "Sorry again. Thought that was it. Just remembered. There's one more question if you don't mind?"

And being helpful to the elderly lady Briony told her to go ahead and ask.

"Er, can you give me your work's number please? Have to have it in case we need to contact you and you're out, y'know what I mean."

She chuckled and wrote down the number Briony was telling her.

The call ended and Briony felt sorry for the old lady getting so flummoxed like that. Reminded her of her own mother.

Now all Jack's team had to do was have the line tapped.

5

A month after Bev had started working in the souvenir-cum-paper shop, she was finding the job interesting. Whilst there was plenty to do, serving the customers, stock-taking, re-ordering, washing up, then, making more coffee than she ever dreamed of, she enjoyed being in such a stress-free environment.

She didn't say anything about it to Briony, but she did tell her how amazed she was at the amount she was being paid. Briony chuckled at that.

It was quite early in the afternoon when Bev heard her boss's landline ringing in the stock room. So, when she let her know, Briony immediately asked her to take over serving a customer whilst she dashed into the back room to answer the call. Briony was smiling to herself, knowing straight away from the time of the call who it was.

"Coming to see me then?" the man asked her. "Usual time and place OK?"

Briony smiled, muttering a simple OK.

She put the phone back in its stand and walked slowly back into the shop. Then, looking at her not-so-scruffy Bev she asked, "If I give you the shop's keys can I trust you lock up tonight for me?"

The face Bev pulled told Briony that she really didn't want to. Probably meant having to get up earlier than normal. *What's wrong with people these days?* she thought, but she knew Bev would do it. Course she would. She wasn't long out of prison. Needed the cash, didn't she?

"Got to have a day off now and again," Briony joked and flicked the switch on the kettle to make some more coffee.

"Going somewhere nice then?" Bev asked dreamily, staring blankly at a plastic model of tower-bridge that she was holding in her hands.

"Visiting a couple of men I know," she replied. Then, pouring the boiling water into two mugs, she winked at Bev, making her smile.

"Lucky you," she laughed.

And at the end of the day Briony tossed the shop keys to Bev, telling her she'd see her in the morning.

"Enjoy yourself then," Bev said, adding, "and don't do anything I wouldn't do."

Briony giggled at the thought, then, before she left the shop, she asked Bev if she'd be good enough and drop the keys back at her flat. She knew from Bev's address it was on her way home.

At first, Bev hesitated, but then nodded her head.

"Oops sorry Bev. Forgot to tell you, there's a security lock on the front door."

Bev sighed while Briony found a piece of paper and began writing.

"That's the number just in case you forget it."

She passed the scribbled note to Bev, who looked at it then screwed it up and put it in her jeans pocket.

"Oh yes, and my flat's on the second floor. Number five. It's the key with the green label on it."

Bev smiled and told her boss it'd be OK.

6

The following Monday morning, not long after Bev had taken Briony's keys back to her flat, a smart-looking middle-aged man in a dark-blue suit strode purposefully down the road where Briony lived, looking at each building in turn as he walked along the pavement, as if he had a particular building in mind. He suddenly stopped outside the large three-storey block of flats and, looking at the small notebook that he'd taken from one of his jacket pockets, he checked the address with the one that was in the book.

Singing to himself as he walked up to the large red wooden door, his fingers pressed the four numbers of the coded security lock. And seconds later, after hearing the sound of the lock being released, he pushed the door open and went inside.

The man was from the landlord's property agency and was delivering letters to the occupiers of the flats in the building, informing the occupier of each flat that some of the landlord's men would be carrying out a quick inspection to determine which flat was or wasn't in need of re-decorating. The letters said that the work would be done whether the occupiers of the flats were in or out, and that the men wouldn't take very long.

Half an hour later and the smartly dressed man made sure the large door of the block of flats was securely locked behind him. He looked up and down the street, then across it, smiling at a woman who'd been sitting in her car on the opposite side of the road with a map of London spread out across the dashboard.

She returned the smile and drove away as the man walked back down the road, looking again at his notebook for the next address he was visiting.

7

During all this time, whenever Briony left the shop in Bev's capable hands, a couple of Jack's team followed her. She was only going to see her estranged English father and his friend. She loved her father more dearly than her mother, especially after their divorce. He was in a nursing home in Woolwich. And the journeys Jack's team made weren't in vain. They now had lots of photos of this suspected terrorist.

In the souvenir shop one Friday morning when Briony was out, the phone rang and when Bev answered it a man told her he'd call back later when she got back. Bev duly passed the message on as she usually did. She was going to make a note of the number when it came up on its screen, but she couldn't because it was from a call box in Euston station.

When Briony took the call later on, she knew who it was from. It was always on a Friday. And it was always from a call box.

"Wednesday afternoon. OK?" the voice whispered.

Briony nodded as if the caller could actually see her. But she said nothing. A reply was not required. That was the arrangement. Unless there was a problem. Then she'd have said anything that came into her head.

She lowered the phone down very slowly and drew a circle round the date on the calendar that hung on the wall near the phone.

8

It wasn't long after the letters from the landlord's property agency had been delivered that an old dirty-white van pulled up and parked in the narrow lane behind the block of flats. It was 10 a.m. A few minutes later and three guys in paint-splattered overalls clambered out. When they finished smoking their cigarettes and cracking jokes, they ground the fag ends into the road, looking as though they were at last going to get some work done.

One of them then rummaged inside the van and took out an old dented metal case. The second guy tugged the end of his baseball hat further down before he pulled out a large, heavy-duty canvas works bag and threw it over one shoulder, whilst the third man, presumably the boss, waited, stuck a pencil behind his ear, and tucked a clipboard under one of his arms. He checked something on the clipboard, nodded towards the entrance of the building, then they all went into the block of flats through the door at the back.

From there these three men from the landlord's decorating services moved swiftly up the stairs and straight to Briony's flat, where, after having completed their work there, they went back down the stairs, closed the small back door, got in their van, and drove away, leaving clouds of exhaust smoke hanging about in the lane.

There were now more bugs in Briony's flat than you'd find in a Moscow hotel.

And for the last seven days, having left her flat in the early morning, Briony had been travelling the three stops from Holborn to Charing Cross, including the one change of line, before finally walking to the small tourist souvenir shop in Whitehall, totally unaware that everything she said and did in her flat was now being watched and listened to by none other than the UK's Secret Intelligence Services.

9

By the middle of October, the intelligence services had gathered more information about Briony and her friends, and because she'd been back and forth to her home in Dublin to meet another friend, the operation was controlled by MI6.

It was Jack's team that became responsible for carrying out eyes-on surveillance, hoping that any day soon Briony and her friends could be picked up, taken somewhere secure and quietly interrogated.

The day began just like any other day in the UK's capital, except that on one of its crowded streets three people were now following Briony.

On one side of the road were Fiona and Greg, with Jack following on the opposite side. Along the street they leap-frogged each other as they kept up with her, crossing the road when they felt the need and sometimes doing a bit of 'dry-cleaning' to make sure *they* weren't being followed as well.

Moving casually among the crowds of people on the street, Briony blended in, but still she had no idea that she was being followed.

When she eventually entered the underground Jack sent a message to a helicopter unit asking them if they could keep watch for her leaving any of the possible underground stations in case they lost contact. It was a big if, even though they had the latest photos of Briony, having watched her from the air before she disappeared into the station.

Unfortunately for Briony, she'd made more phone calls and she'd spoken about more weapons coming from Dublin, which threw

Jack's office into a flap and created a buzz of excitement for those watching her.

10

Wednesday morning arrived and with their earphones plugged into what looked like their mobiles, Jack's team looked just like any one of the hundreds of people on their way to work as each of them entered the underground station at Holborn.

However, once inside, Briony didn't go for her usual train on the Piccadilly line. Instead, she headed for the Central line, west bound, and Jack had to alert the helicopter team in the air above central London that she was changing her route.

They'd already been informed she wasn't going to work, but what they didn't know was where she was heading and, more important, who she was meeting.

Once Jack's team was on the train, communication was with no one else other than each other, via the throat-mikes they were wearing, hidden under the collars of their coats.

When the train arrived in the station, Greg followed Briony into the same carriage, standing almost shoulder to shoulder with her.

Jack was halfway down the carriage behind and Fiona was right at the end, watching the team's six. Keeping them all safe.

Everything was going to plan.

Unfortunately though, the surveillance was suddenly brought to an abrupt end, aborted when the train was ripped apart by a bomb just after it had left the station, leaving over thirty people dead and many more seriously injured.

11

News of the bombing spread like wildfire throughout the entire media and everything in the city went in another direction. There were now more serious tasks for all of the security services to be getting on with.

Those who knew what Jack's team were doing were left wondering if they might have been on the same train and wanted to learn what they could about their friends. And whilst they were now busily trying to find out anything about the terrorists, none of them had any idea if their friends were alive or not. It's such times as these that life can really be very unforgiving.

They knew some people would be collecting and sifting through the list of any survivors who ended up in hospital, hoping and praying that their colleagues were still alive and safe.

For now though, they were tasked with leaving no stone unturned in their quest to bring them nearer to this other terrorist cell which, until that day, had been totally below their radar.

*

In a house in Kilburn Connor waited. He was Briony's brother and every minute or so he kept looking at his watch. He was getting anxious. She was late. Very late. He kept going to the front room and peering through the net curtains, hoping that he'd catch sight of her walking up the road.

He went back to the kitchen and made himself a coffee. His third one that morning. He wanted to call Brendan and Sean, but he knew he couldn't do that. Ever. Especially not from there.

Wandering around the large house he wrung his hands, worrying, fretting, wondering what to do. *Where the hell is she?* he kept asking himself.

He went upstairs to get a better view from the bedroom window, but the road was just the same. Empty.

Briony was nowhere to be seen and Connor knew it wasn't like her. So, to take his mind off her he switched the radio on.

'. . . there are lots of casualties and the emergency services have told us they don't know yet just how many of those on the train have been killed.'

Connor's face turned pale.

"Holy Mother of God!" he screamed, letting the news on the radio sink in. "Please don't let her be one of them."

12

On the train Jack was watching from across the gap where the carriages joined. His colleague Greg in the other carriage was standing shoulder to shoulder with Briony, nodding his head as though listening to music through his headset and unbelievably at one point he actually exchanged a few words as well.

It's not a bad thing that people never really know who they are standing next to. Never should either. If the job's done correctly.

However, Greg and Briony were too far away to have been seriously injured and eventually, after the explosion, hours later when London's underground network's electricity supply was safely switched off, allowing the rescue teams to gain access, kill the flames that were filling the tunnels with very dense, toxic smoke and reach the injured, Briony was helped off the train by one of the emergency services' teams. She was one of the lucky ones.

Lucky for a second time that day, because after being examined by medical staff at one of the many emergency casualty triage tents that were speedily erected in nearby streets she was eventually treated for minor cuts and bruises and given the all clear. She gave her name and address to the medics, smiling and thanking them for what they'd done, then she kissed the small silver cat that hung with the other nick-knacks that dangled from the strap on her handbag. Knew then how lucky she really was.

Greg also escaped the bombing similarly unscathed. Unfortunately, though, a different rescue team got him out of the carriage and he ended up in another treatment facility. In another street. And whilst those above ground were now no longer looking for Briony, the surveillance team below had by then lost all contact with her.

Tragically, Fiona was killed in the blast along with those who were standing next to the young suicide bomber.

13

"Bloody hell girl, what the fuck's happened to you?"

Briony looked at her brother, sighed deeply, and gave him a weak smile when he met her at the front door of the house.

"You weren't caught in that b …?"

Limping into the front room she nodded her head, answering his question before he finished it and flopped down heavily onto the old sofa.

"Only just managed to get a fuckin' taxi."

Connor locked the door quickly and followed her into the lounge. He still couldn't believe what had happened. He was looking almost as if *he'd* been on the train. Perhaps it was the shock of seeing Briony in that state? He was thinking of the consequences of what his friends were planning.

"I can't get my head round it all, Briony. It's bloody terrible," he exclaimed. "Now let me get you a cup of something."

She shook her head slowly, closed her eyes, and released the anger that had built up after her ordeal. Her body shook uncontrollably and tears began to pour down her cheeks.

Shock was coming out.

Connor went into the kitchen and made a cup of tea, adding a large drop of Irish whiskey to it. He sat down with her and handed her the mug.

"Drink this, girl. It'll make you feel a lot better."

Smiling appreciatively, she took the cup from him, steadying it in both hands whilst she sipped the tea. She sniffed a couple of times and said thanks.

The fact that Briony had been injured in a bombing was bringing home the reality of what they were hoping to do themselves.

And it was troubling him.

"Sean'll be here about six o'clock, so relax on the sofa and finish your drink. I'll leave you be," he told her.

14

After the bombing, the media of course reported that it had been carried out by a group of unknown terrorists, criticising the security services for not having known about them. What they couldn't find out they made up, filling the pages with speculation and fake news. TV reporters stood in front of the cameras asking the same senile questions too, dramatizing the same stories and showing the same footage from the scene around the entrance to Holborn's underground station every few minutes.

And for once, even the country's boring politics were kicked to one side and, thankfully, to the relief of the entire country, taken off the air for quite a few days.

The emergency services were naturally given lots of airtime though, as was the Prime Minister, who lavished her praises on all the men and women who'd helped treat the injured. Vowing that those responsible would be caught and brought to justice, and hopefully, given very long terms in prison, she continued to raise everyone's hopes. She always did that. But they were false hopes. Hardly ever happened. Perhaps by saying it made her feel strong. As if she were in command. The leader.

And that was her failing.

Daphne Blakemoor was the weakest and most hated Prime Minister the country had ever known.

15

A ball of fire swept through the train and Jack was caught in it. Burnt from the tops of his shoulders right down to his backside. Most of his clothes were blown off in the blast, but those that remained were burning into what was once the skin on his back.

He was facing forward, with his back to the unknown girl who carried the bomb in her backpack, and as the train left the station its passengers were jolted a few times, throwing its standing passengers backwards.

Over-compensating for it, Jack leaned forward a bit. But *that* bit was just when the woman detonated her bomb. And being in the centre of the carriage Jack was close enough to get burnt.

Badly burnt.

Fiona, on the other hand, was standing next to the young suicide bomber and when the train shook its passengers as it left the station she just happened to look down. Saw the young woman slowly pulling a mobile phone from out of her backpack. Noticed the paint tins hidden inside it. And disappearing into the woman's backpack was the thin lead from her phone.

In the second she saw it Fiona could neither shout a warning nor stop the girl. Everything around her slowed down and became unreal. The world went silent. She watched helplessly as the woman closed her eyes and began to tremble. Watched her lips moving silently as though she were saying a prayer. Looked on horrified as the girl's thumb found the top of her mobile and slowly pressed a key. The bomb was an amateur home-made device, but it was successful.

Two empty litre paint tins were filled with a mixture of concentrated washing-up liquid and petrol which produced something similar to napalm, albeit the cheap version. And amongst the thick liquid were nuts, bolts, and shards of thick glass. Plus a few tea-spoonfuls of rat poison.

A tiny amount of C4 explosive, plus a detonator, was attached to the tins, allowing the girl holding the mobile to make the simple but final contact when she pressed any key, sending the electric current down the wire at extraordinary speed and causing the bomb to explode, spewing its thick lethal flaming contents on anything in its way.

And Jack caught more of it than he realised.

Amidst the broken glass, the burnt shredded pieces of wood, the molten plastic, and the twisted metal wreckage of the train, Jack's motionless body lay there with others for what must have been hours, until finally the rescue teams were able to reach him.

They'd eventually found him crumpled up against some pieces of blackened bent steel that looked like a large piece of modern art. However, *that* had once been the doors of the carriage he was near.

Hidden under burning seats and splintered wood from the floor he looked just like another lump. Another shape. But a badly burnt shape.

His back was raw. His flesh was wet. Tissue and burnt skin that were still attached were bleeding. Oozing. Smouldering. And in the back of his left leg was a piece of hot metal. So hot that it had cauterized the blood and stopped him losing any more.

Jack was unconscious. Didn't move. Couldn't. Didn't speak. Couldn't. And his life was ebbing away second by second.

The carnage that the suicide bomber had caused was invisible to him. All the damage the bomb had done to the train and station was unseen. The mangled bodies of the dead whose limbs had been horrendously ripped apart would not be in his nightmares. Neither would the screams of the injured or the shouts of the survivors and their rescuers. And the smell of death aboard that train was never in his nostrils.

16

It was getting dark by the time Sean arrived at the large house along Priory Park Road in Kilburn and after Connor had told him about Briony's lucky escape he ran into the lounge where she was sleeping.

"Briony," he cried as he shook her shoulder, "thank God you're still alive!"

She stirred, half asleep, wondering what was happening, trying to figure out where she was. And through bleary half-closed eyes she saw his face. And he looked upset. She blinked a few times and slowly sat up.

"She got caught in that underground bombing, m'friend," Connor told him again, by which time Sean was slowly sitting down and putting one of his arms round her shoulders.

Handing him a tumbler of whiskey, Connor looked at Briony.

"Come back to Bristol with me tonight, sis, and stay for a while."

It was only a suggestion, but Briony nodded her head. And without realising it he became instrumental in keeping her safe in more ways than one.

"It'll do you good to get away from it too. We'll arrange for someone to run the shop so Bev isn't on her own as well, OK?"

"But I've nothing to wear, Con, my clothes are all in the flat. I only have what I stand up in."

"Don't worrying about that, girl. We've always got some for times like this and once you're in Bristol, we'll put you in a spa for a couple of days too. It'll make you feel like a new woman, believe me."

She nodded and they all moved from the front room and went into the back room to talk about their next move.

17

After being rescued Jack was rushed to one of the many hospitals that were on the emergency stand-by list for such disastrous incidents as this.

Days later, still unconscious, his very soul was crying out. Its cries were silent, painful ones. And if he'd been conscious, he'd have known just how much pain he was in.

By then his colleagues knew that Greg was alive, but Fiona wasn't. They also knew where Jack was and what state he was in.

Machines monitored his progress. Tubes down his raw throat were connected to other machines. Air was delivered for him to breathe. Helped him breathe. Made him breathe.

Tubes fed liquids into his fragile body. Others drained some out. People around him busily attended to his needs. The other victims who were nearby were treated just the same.

Jack was looked at every ten or fifteen minutes. Lives were discussed by consultants who were making decisions to keep him and those like him alive.

Staff dressed the burnt areas as best they could. They'd only feel the pain after their shifts were finished. But Jack would only ever find out how intense his pain was once he regained consciousness.

If he did.

It was all he knew for the first twelve weeks whilst teams of surgeons, doctors, and nurses gradually eased some of the pain, raising his hopes of some sort of recovery. But the pain never left him.

Eighteen months after the bombing, one of the specialists told him how due to wars and incidents like the one he'd experienced, medical science had moved forward in leaps and bounds, improving all the time, producing methods of preserving life that ten years before would have seemed impossible, but Jack wasn't that sure, because after several skin-grafts he found nothing had taken away any of the most agonising pain he was in.

He welcomed the many visits he had from those he worked with, but Jack realised he may not be allowed back when his treatment was finished. And *that* saddened him.

After more operations and hours of physio Jack was given full use of his badly injured body.

And two years after the bombing, fully recovered, he was told to take leave and given a temporary medical discharge with full pay. He was still on the books of course, in case he wanted to go back, but, they said, if he did, and because of his leg injury, it might only be a desk job.

Jack was now faced with hoping to stay with MI6 or reluctantly leave it.

A couple of weeks later he made his decision, he moved to Bristol. He got a new job near Barton Hill. Accounts manager for a small local family-run delivery service.

But the only things he was left with were the unforgettable memories, the nightmares, the flashbacks, the very nasty scars, the aching shoulders, the limp and, most of all, the grief of losing Fiona, his very good friend and dedicated colleague.

Jack thought it very ironic that one faceless group of terrorists had unknowingly saved the life of another of their ilk.

18

Not long after Jack moved to Bristol, he was happily walking to the Watershed one Saturday to meet a woman he'd recently made friends with and his shoulders began to ache.

The sky was heavy with darkening thunder clouds, and it looked like rain. He remembered the medics telling him his shoulders would ache whenever it rained, so he rubbed them, warming them, soothing them, just like they'd advised.

He was making his way along St Augustine's Parade towards the Watershed in Bristol, when he noticed people gathering near Neptune's statue, where, lining up, was what looked like a military parade of some sort. Pieces of artillery were already on display and for those who wanted to get a closer look a Mortar, a GPMG and a small mine-detector were waiting to be handled under the supervisory eyes of one of the soldiers. Rearing up next to these weapons was a climbing-wall with thick ropes from the top of it for kids of all ages to enjoy the short exciting death-slide.

The Army was recruiting.

A voice boomed out.

"Squaaaaad! . . . Squaad, shun!"

The crunch of boots on the flagstones sounded as one. It made the hairs on Jack's neck stand up, filling his mind with memories from when he'd been in the Army Cadet Force at university a long time ago. He smiled to himself when he saw the Mayor with some of his dignitaries making a brief inspection of those hosting the show.

Jack walked on.

And continuing along the street, the thought of one of the Royal Navy's nuclear submarines suddenly popping up in the Watershed brought a smile to his face. He chuckled. If only.

He'd just gone past the Hippodrome when, after a very loud clap of thunder, the heavens opened and it began to pour down. Stair rods weren't the words. So, looking for shelter, Jack turned right and darted up Denmark Street as best he could.

He almost went into a cafe called You & Meow, which had real cats inside, some idling away their time sleeping in the windows, others being stroked by the customers. But before he got there, he spotted a cafe on the other side of the street, nearer, and dashing across to it he went inside, out of the rain.

It was quite a small place and there were only three people in it to begin with. The first one, an elderly lady in a thin blue raincoat, was sitting by the window, staring into the street as the large drops of rain tried and failed to wash the grime off the window.

The second, a bloke who looked about sixty but was probably much younger, was lolling on the bench seat that was against the wall at the back of the cafe.

Facing the door, he looked quite at home there with his arms spread out across the back of the seat. He was relaxed, but he looked as though he didn't have a penny to his name. His clothes were worn out and grimy from probably sleeping rough and, from the needle marks up his arms, Jack knew he'd been shooting heroin or some other drug. And the third person, presumably the cafe's owner, was behind the counter that ran along most of the left side of the cafe.

Wearing an off-white long-sleeved shirt and jeans under his greasy apron he was wiping some cutlery with an old piece of cloth that had seen better days.

Jack got a smile that showed a few blackened teeth when he

ordered a hot chocolate and paid for it. Then, after putting it on a table near the counter, he nipped to the loo through a door at the back of the cafe.

He'd just come back along the short corridor from the loo, was about to put a hand round the doorknob and go back into the cafe when an angry voice at the other side of the door made him stay where he was.

"Well, well, well. If it isn't Eddie."

And BOOM!

Someone screamed. Probably the elderly lady. The noise was very loud and reverberated through the cafe. And Jack knew it hadn't been thunder.

A weapon had just been fired.

Quite a while since he'd heard a noise like that and in such a confined space it had partially deafened him.

Quickly pressing his face against the gap in the doorjamb to see what was happening, he heard the owner's muffled voice inside the cafe shout, "What the fu—?" But he didn't get the words out.

BOOM!

More screams.

And for a few seconds there was nothing to see. Just smoke. Then, a man ran out of the cafe.

Still waving the gun in his hand he suddenly turned and looked back. Jack saw the gunman's face and it frightened him for a moment or two, because from where he was standing, Jack thought the guy was looking directly at *him*. As though he knew Jack was standing there behind the door.

As if he knew exactly who Jack was.

19

A couple of weeks after the bombing Bev was told to hand her notice in. Tell the woman who'd replaced Briony that she'd got another job and to thank her very much for giving her another start after her term in prison. When she did, the woman shrugged her shoulders, mentioned that she didn't have to work any notice and wrote out her P45. Any money owing to her would go into her bank on Friday. Thank you.

Meanwhile, at home in Bristol, Sean had just come through the door from his kitchen carrying two mugs of coffee.

"Brendan, for fuck's sake, why didn't you wait until he was on his own somewhere bloody quiet and not there in town?"

Brendan sneered viciously at his friend but understood what was being said.

"Had to take him out as soon as I could. Got a loose tongue and he's been on the drugs again. Can't have someone like him with us, Sean. Never know what he'd do next."

His friend shook his head, still not sure that the cafe was the best place to have killed the guy.

"OK," he replied. "It's just that we'll have to keep our friggin' heads down now, eh? Jesus Brendan man, if you carry on like that, we'll be afraid to step outside."

Brendan knew what his friend was saying. He took a sip of his coffee.

"Let's not argue about it, Sean. It's done now and that's all that matters."

20

Having rung the emergency services, the cafe owner was having trouble because the noise from the shooting had frightened and temporarily deafened him. And the smoke from the weapon was making him cough. Made Jack cough too. Meanwhile, outside, a few people who'd been in the street were gawping through the cafe's windows wondering what had happened.

The guy sitting at the back of the cafe had been shot twice. Killed. Looked pretty obvious to Jack but none of the others in the cafe knew it just then.

Jack looked at those gathering outside in the pouring rain, he wondered why they were so interested. Most were just standing there, pointing at the guy who'd been shot. Some of them even had their mobile phones out. For God's sake!

The victim, however, was slouched in his seat against the wall. Head back, chin up. Jack knew he wasn't going to need any treatment though. The red stain spreading across his already grubby shirt-front confirmed that. Dark frothy blood was still congealing in his mouth, down his chin, and onto his front like an erupting volcano whose lava was cooling, before going crusty and hardening when it could go no further. And from the position of his body Jack reckoned *that* had been the first shot.

The other one had struck him under his left eye, throwing his head, or what was left of it, back as far as it would go, leaving most of it splattered across the once almost white-tiled wall behind him.

The elderly lady was holding a hanky to her ashen face, sobbing and shaking. At first, Jack thought she was having a heart attack, but she wasn't. Shock was setting in. And nudging the owner, Jack mimed drinking a cup of something. He got the owner to make her a cup of tea.

He shouted to tell him not to touch anything as well and as he went back to his seat, he carefully stepped round the two empty 9mm brass cases that were lying motionless on the floor. Dare say the police would find one round stuck somewhere in the back of the dead guy's seat and the other with the remnants of the guy's brains that now decorated the wall.

Within minutes though, two police cars screeched to a halt outside the cafe. Blue and red lights were flashing on and off as though a fuse was about to blow. Then, before anyone came inside the cafe, a riot van drew up as well and the small crowd outside moved back very quickly.

Cops were everywhere. Jack hadn't seen so many for a long time. Those in uniform were moving the crowd further away. Others were tying blue and white police tapes across parts of the street whilst two or three more were doing the same thing further up it. An armed response unit arrived but left minutes later after being told they weren't required. By then, chatter over the airwaves was melting the networks.

A young policewoman was holding the old lady's hand, comforting her whilst quietly asking her some questions and sitting at an empty table, the owner of the cafe was trying to make sense of what had just happened. Then, sitting down where Jack had left his hot drink, one of the detectives joined him.

But before Jack had a chance to say anything to the detective, an ambulance arrived. Its flashing lights illuminated the wet pavements outside as well as the smoke that was still hanging about inside the cafe and because the cafe's radio above the counter was playing music, it gave the place the appearance of a seedy down-and-out night-club.

The medics ran in and looked at the dead guy, muttered something to each other and whilst one of them began to check the old lady out, the other asked the owner if he was OK.

By this time Jack's hearing was almost back to normal and the detective was asking him what he'd seen. So he told him.

"Bloody great," he smirked when he'd finished writing down what Jack had had to say.

"Won't be needing much evidence now," he told him.

Jack nodded and the detective thanked him.

"Murder it is then," he chuckled to himself.

Wasn't fuckin' suicide was it? Jack thought.

The detective called to one of the others in plain clothes and handed him a plastic bag to put some evidence in. He'd got Jack's name, address, and landline number. He told him he'd go round to his place later that day to ask more questions. Reckoned Jack should then go home. Not speak to anyone about what he'd seen.

The old lady was helped out of the cafe to the ambulance whilst Jack listened to the detective's advice. Then, four people clad from head to toe in white paper-like clothes and wearing white nose-masks came shuffling in through the door. Move out of the way. Scene of crime officers.

Minutes later a shiny black van arrived and parked behind one of the police cars in the street. Probably from the morgue to collect the body after all the photos had been taken.

And Jack got up to go.

But as he reached the cafe's front door, a newspaper photographer's camera flashed in his face. He didn't like his photo being taken, so he hurried back towards the Watershed as quickly as he could with the face of the gunman now unforgettably chiselled in his mind.

What Jack didn't notice as he hurried back towards the Watershed was a man in a dark-blue hoodie nipping under the police tapes on the other side of the street. Didn't see the man hurrying up the street, on the other side of the road, going in the opposite direction.

An hour or so later, when the detective came to see him, Jack was told that because of the evidence he'd supplied, he might receive threats from the gunman's friends. Didn't sound good. Didn't happen though. Not then.

The detective also mentioned that there'd been a mugging further up the street near Denmark Avenue. Joked that it wasn't the right place to be that day.

The following morning, on his way to see a friend, Jack had bought the local paper and opening it he was very surprised to see the printed headlines across the front page.

LOCAL MAN WITNESSES MURDER IN CAFE!

Jack was relieved not to see his face there but wondered why, knowing that he'd been photographed leaving the cafe, but what he was most annoyed about was seeing his name in print.

*

"Brendan! It's for you."

Passing the phone to him, Sean waited until the conversation had ended. Something had excited his friend. He'd seen Brendan's face light up. And to have done that had made him wonder what the call was about, because Brendan hardly ever smiled.

Puffing his cheeks out and slowly blowing his breath from out of them Brendan suddenly punched the air with one hand.

"Yessssss!" he shouted.

"What's up, mate?"

"Uncle Michael's got the perfect place for us. Said it'll be difficult for anyone to find, but it'd be up and running soon. Said it'll be a very safe too."

And opening a couple of cans of Guinness, Brendan handed one to his friend.

"This calls for a celebration, Sean. Things are getting better, mate."

Raising his can of Guinness to Brendan, Sean nodded his head, silently thinking that they would be, so long as Brendan didn't shoot anyone else.

21

Unbeknown to Jack when he left the cafe, the man in the hoodie had followed the photographer who was heading for a pint in the Hatchet Inn and just as he reached Frogmore Street he was hit hard in the back and knocked down onto the ground.

Dazed and wondering what the hell had just happened, the photographer watched his assailant disappear. Then, a moment later, he realised his camera had also disappeared.

By the time the mugger had got to College Green he slowed down to a walking pace, lost the wet, dark-blue top he'd been wearing minutes before and now looked like anyone else that afternoon carrying a Tesco carrier bag, only this bag contained the stolen camera wrapped up in the top he'd just discarded.

He dumped the bag in a rubbish bin at the back of the Watershed, walked across Pero's Bridge to Prince Street and caught a bus to take him back to his car at the Long Ashton Park & Ride.

Once there he put the camera's SD card into his small laptop, fired it up, and looked at the photos that were on it.

Minutes later only the last photo remained.

*

"Since we're having to keep our heads down, Brendan, are you still going to find that bloke in the papers then?"

He waited a few moments, watching Brendan running it through his mind.

"Not us m'friend, Connor and Pat. They'll sort it out."

Sean laughed, hoping it wouldn't take too long. After all, they had more important things to get on with.

"They're away on holiday in Ireland arranging things at the moment, but I'll see them when they get back."

"What're you going to have them do then?"

"What d'you think?" he chuckled. "Just have them rough him up a bit. But not too much, else we'll have the entire police force looking for us."

Sean knew what he meant.

"Mmmm, so long as the family don't start doing their own things though eh?"

"They probably will, Sean, but it'll not concern us m'friend, will it?"

22

But before Brendan was caught, things *did* begin to kick-off and that
was when Jack found out just how nasty Brendan's family and friends
really were. One of Jack's neighbours had seen Jack's name in the
paper and, being a friend of Sean's, he told them exactly where Jack
lived.

After that Jack began to receive anonymous threatening letters.

He changed the landline number, also bought a new mobile with a
new number, but somehow the odd anonymous phone call came
through. Seemed that Brendan had friends in all sorts of places.

By then, Jack and his partner Fran were getting really fed up from
the letters he received, telling him what a scumbag he was and that
Fran was a whore. 'The Fuckin' Mattress of Bristol' one letter called
her. Then, when his car's windscreen and lights were smashed one
evening in Asda's car park, he let the police know, but they said it
was probably just local vandalism, because that night other cars in the
same car park were damaged as well.

He realised then how Brendan's friends knew how to cover their
arses.

Jack felt that the police were turning a blind eye to it, until later,
after complaining that a couple of firelighters and a cat's head
smeared in shit had been pushed through their letter box, as well as
all four tyres on his car being slashed, it was only then that they told
him they'd take it more seriously.

A couple of days later, however, Jack's mood changed for the
better when he got a phone call from a woman at the police station

to ask if she could visit them for a chat that evening and offer them some counselling.

She told him her name was Val and that she'd be at their place at 7.15 p.m.

"I'll call you on your landline. I'll just let it ring three times," she explained, "then you'll know it's me. If you give me your e-mail address, I'll send you my picture so you'll recognise me as well."

Jack did as he'd been asked and within a few seconds her photo was in his phone.

That night Jack and Fran waited to hear what Val was going to say to them; what advice she was able to give them; how she could go about making them feel that little bit safer.

And at 7.15 precisely, the phone rang. Jack heard it ring three times and, looking at the photo of Val in his phone, he went to the door with Fran following just after she'd rung the bell.

But as he opened it Fran suddenly screamed.

And Jack froze.

23

Although the person at the door was a woman, might have even been called Val for all Jack knew, she looked nothing like the photo in his phone. Half of her face was covered with what looked like a white plastic mask. Looked a bit like the Phantom of the Opera.

Standing about two yards away, in her dark green anorak and jeans, the woman's left arm was stretched straight out in front of her, steady as a rock and Jack found himself staring right into the barrel of a gun.

His heart missed several beats as he waited for a round to punch a hole in him somewhere. He held his breath. And in total panic his heart was pushing his blood through his veins with the force of a high-pressure hose, making a pulsating sound like that of escaping steam hiss loudly in his ears. Then he saw the woman expertly pull the slider back and load the weapon. Saw her finger slowly move towards the trigger. Watched the woman raise her arm slightly.

Behind her mask she closed her right eye and looked down the short barrel, lining it up with Jack's head that was now fully before her in her sights, just a few feet away.

To Jack it seemed a lifetime waiting for the muzzle flash, not that he'd have seen its result or felt the pain, unless she wasn't a good shot. And at that distance she didn't need to be good. He saw her finger curl round the trigger, and he closed his eyes waiting for the final end.

But the gun was empty. And all he heard was the hollow click of the gun's hammer striking the empty chamber, where normally a live round would have been waiting to make the kill.

That made him feel much worse than if he'd been shot. And as the woman ran off, shouting that she'd get him next time, Jack recognised the voice that only a couple of hours earlier had told him she'd visit and counsel them. But it also reminded him of another voice from the past.

Then he started to throw up.

After what happened, he immediately rang the police. Fran was in shock and he was angry with himself. Should've known better. Knew it wouldn't have happened years ago. Should've sussed it out straight away. Knew then that he was losing it. Promised himself it wouldn't happen again. Felt a complete prick falling for that old bloody trick. Should've asked for Val's number to phone her back.

The police tried to calm them both down, telling them there'd be some surveillance in place around their home, but when Jack asked them what next, suggesting Brendan's family might plant a bomb under his car, they only looked at each other and shrugged their shoulders.

"All I want," Jack protested angrily, "is to be left in peace. Not fuckin' pieces!"

24

"Heard Briony was giving that bloke some hassle the other night then?"

It wasn't a question that needed answering, just a statement of fact, but Brendan replied all the same.

"Mmm. Trouble is she thinks *she* can sort it out and might start doing stupid things. I'll have to have words with her."

Then he laughed.

"But she sure must have worried him a bit. Heard the police were swarming all over the place afterwards."

They both chuckled as they looked at a couple of weapons that Brendan had recently taken delivery of.

"Getting more of these soon, m'friend," he said as he unwrapped one of the weapons from the waxed paper that it had been in.

"Getting more explosives too," he added as he felt the gun's weight in his hand, balancing it before pretending to fire it.

"What?" Sean asked in surprise, looking at the new weapon in his friend's hand.

Brendan smiled, nodded, and pointed the greasy new Glock 17 at a picture they used as a dart board which hung on the back of the door.

Daphne Blakemoor's face was covered in lots of holes.

*

Anyone in the Bristol area who'd read the local paper would have seen the story of the murder in the cafe in Denmark Street. Some of the readers might have even read the couple of paragraphs on page four about the mugging near there too, but to most people who read the papers, they were only two more stories in the news that would most likely be forgotten after a couple of days.

However, to one man the main story was very important. So important that before Jack's photo reached the press, he'd made sure it didn't.

When he hurried up Denmark Street, he'd seen Jack leaving the cafe. Recognised him. Knew him. Used to work together. But he couldn't contact him there. Not then.

He'd had to go to a meeting in one of the cafes in Cribbs Causeway to finalise the details of a job he was on and having to go to Dublin that day hadn't left him time to read the Bristol papers.

25

Having been caught, Brendan O'Shea sat with his brief, going over the sequence of events that had led him to being in that cell, charged with murder.

"But there wasn't another bloke in the cafe!" he complained, shouting at his brief.

"There was," confirmed his well-spoken lawyer, "but you didn't see him."

"So where the fuck was he then?" Brendan screamed and in a violent rage of disbelief he thumped the table.

The lawyer looked boringly over his specs at him and raised one eyebrow. He'd heard it all before.

"Transpires," he announced, as if bored to death, "that he was in the corridor between the toilets and the door into the cafe."

Brendan frowned. Puzzled. Hadn't really seen a door to the loo. His hands were slowly squeezing into fists. He still didn't understand.

"What?" he shouted. "So how come he bloody saw me then?"

His brief sighed a long, slow, and silent 'oh dear' whilst flicking through his notes.

Adjusting his specs, he looked across the table at Brendan.

"He used his mobile phone and videoed you leaving the cafe waving the gun in your hand," he explained as he put his papers back into his briefcase. "Got you full-face too."

The sound of Brendan's lawyer snapping shut his briefcase echoed in the empty cell, sending a shiver down Brendan's spine. Reality had just touched a nerve. And for the first time in his life Brendan was frightened.

As his brief got up to leave, he looked at his client.

"It means, Mr O'Shea, that the only plea you can now make is going to be that of guilty. And I don't think it'll lessen your sentence either."

26

Having just returned from one of his many meetings with the Prime Minister, Sir David Havelock-Price, head of the UK's Secret Intelligence Services, or C as he was known, had decided to have a break instead of taking the lift to his office on the fourth floor. The meeting with Daphne hadn't gone well. It never did. She'd been at his throat again. Wanted to close the rift between the UK and the Republic of Ireland. Forever. To forget the past and rebuild something better for everyone. Sir David knew that would never happen.

And although he knew where she was going, Sir David never trusted any ideas she had that would make her look great. Give her the boost she needed in the public's eyes. Everyone knew she hogged the limelight far too much. No one else's opinions mattered.

So, the meeting had ended with the Prime Minister almost threatening him, saying she would sack him if he didn't go along with her ideas. Didn't do what she told him. Make him resign if she had to. And that, to Sir David, was the last straw. He walked out of the Prime Minister's office, smirking whilst nodding at those who worked at the other side of the PM's doors. Sir David was very much liked by them. He was a popular figure of authority and would, if he could, make her resign instead.

By the time he'd walked back to Vauxhall his anger had subsided, so he walked into the spacious atrium and sat alone at one of the cafeteria's many tables, nursing a cup of black coffee and a piece of chocolate cake. He often went there, usually to get away from his office, and 'that confounded bloody woman' as he called the PM. He found he could relax there, stretch his legs for a few moments and contemplate the many security issues that were being investigated. It also allowed others to see him too.

Those who knew him nodded politely when they passed by, moving quickly away in case questions were raised later. And once word got round that he was there in the cafeteria, and it didn't take long, those who had never met him whispered among themselves, occasionally glancing at him like he was someone you didn't want to be the wrong side of.

But Sir David wasn't the sort of person to make people feel like that, unless of course, they *had* found themselves on his wrong side.

In the cafeteria, however, no one ever approached him. No one ever spoke to him unless it was a matter of life or death such as his wife wanting to speak to him about arrangements for one of her dinners. Nothing ever took place in the cafeteria, apart from a drink and a piece of cake, but should he see someone he wanted to talk to, he'd go sit and chat. Nothing secret. Nothing even classified at the lowest level. Just chat. Like friends. However, should someone want to speak to him, it was *he* who banged the drum. Always a one-way thing.

And as he sipped his coffee, enjoying the short break, he couldn't help overhearing a conversation taking place between two women at the table next to his, and he listened. He knew them both. They worked together in the same department, monitoring the unsavoury phone calls of certain unworthy politicians.

After finishing his coffee and cake, Sir David stood up, took his tray and dirty crockery back to the counter, said thank you to the lady who'd just served him, and strode across the atrium to take the lift back to his office, high above the banks of the Thames.

Fifteen minutes later, after having gone through the remaining day's schedule with his PA, Sir David sat back in his leather chair and asked her to summon one of the women to his office. It was the story she'd been telling that he'd found interesting.

27

After a fight Jack had been in, one that he reckoned was planned by the O'Shea's, he took two weeks off work.

About 10 a.m. the young police officer came around to Jack's home like he'd promised the night before and over a cup of coffee he told the officer what he could remember. Reckoned he'd broken one of the guy's hands. Wasn't sure. Just heard the noise it'd made. The police officer grimaced at the thought. Jack thought the other bloke had worn a ring though and it had someone's initials on it.

The police officer asked how he knew, so carefully peeling the lint dressing off his right cheek Jack showed him the mark it had left.

The copper's mouth dropped open. Only a second. Couldn't believe it.

"Bloody hell! Must've hit you hard," he said sympathetically. "Did you say he was standing in front of you?"

Jack nodded slowly.

The policeman wrote some more details of the fight in his pad, then, after asking Jack's permission, he pulled his mobile phone out and he took a close-up photograph under the dressing of the reddened damaged skin that had been caused by the ring.

It showed the outline of two initials, back to front, which were from the guy's ring. Must have been raised proud, leaving a mark on Jack's cheek for all to see.

"Must have been left-handed then by the looks of it," added the police officer.

Whilst Jack was trying to win the fight there hadn't been much time to think about which hand had hit him. He hadn't given it much thought and he explained that since the two guys had taken quite a beating, he didn't want to press charges because he knew they wouldn't do it again. The copper nodded and a couple of minutes later he left Jack's house.

Getting some time off work sounded great, but Fran decided that she'd had enough and was going to move away. Leave him.

He didn't understand at first. He thought they were an item. But it turned out there was a guy Fran worked with who was shaggin' the arse off her. Stayed late after work and used the desk in the office of her boss, Mrs McBryde.

Jack felt like writing to her, to warn her about the stains she might find on it. *'If you've touched it don't lick y'fingers!'* sort of thing, and thinking about it made him laugh, but it also made his cracked ribs hurt. Felt much better for it though.

And several days later, when he got home from work, Jack found the note. It just said 'gone'. No 'thank you' or 'goodbye'. Fran had left him. Didn't leave an address either. Just disappeared.

So, Jack reckoned he'd do the same. Start again somewhere else.

To get off the map, Jack looked at one. Got his road atlas out, closed his eyes, found a page, and stuck a pin in it. Then, to get the feel of the place he went to where he'd stuck the pin and stayed for a few nights, looking for places to live, finding out how much they'd cost and seeing what sort of jobs were on offer.

Writing dozens of letters, he applied for all sorts of things. He even had several interviews and then he waited.

Until one morning in February when he had a phone call and was offered a job in Staffordshire. So he too disappeared off the radar.

28

After he moved, Jack was thinking about the gun incident with Val. He lay awake quite a few nights going over her voice in his mind. He knew he'd heard it before. Then, one night he suddenly remembered whose it was. He shuddered violently. Tears began to run down his face and curling up into a foetal position he began to weep uncontrollably, remembering all the pain she'd brought.

He rang a number to pass on the information, but a woman's voice only said thank you. It would be looked into. He really hoped someone there would follow it up, but he knew it would be a long shot.

Now living in a three-up, two-down, Jack's terraced-house backed onto the Trent & Mersey Canal. From the lounge he could walk out onto the small patio where, weather permitting, he could have breakfast outside before going to work.

The town was quiet, just like the neighbours on either side of him and just across the road was a Morrisons. Not the biggest, but it served its purpose. Lots of other shops were along the pedestrian precinct too. Forty odd years ago it had been busy with traffic that ran through what used to be this small mining town.

A stone's throw away from Jack's home was a bridge over the canal and beyond it was a new Tesco supermarket. The road over the canal bridge was closed to traffic now as well. And to Jack the place he lived in was perfect.

He'd been living there for just over two years and had taken the position of accounts manager at a small transport company near

Cannock. Ran eight units, trailers, and a small rigid truck.

It wasn't far from one of Amazon's giant distribution centres which gave the company plenty of work, running in and out of it nearly every other day. And night. Filled whatever empty spaces were on the loading schedule, along with the other long-term contracts the company had. Kept the business ticking over and the boss happy. Kept Jack happy too.

It was May and the canal was beginning to look like the M6 in slow motion, but instead of seeing thousands of motor vehicles, colourfully decorated canal-boats were chugging up and down the waterway, slowly navigating their way from there to someplace else.

Swans, ducks, and other water birds were everywhere. Hedgerows had broken out in various shades of green. Birds were singing. Flowers in the parks and gardens were blooming and life for Jack was becoming enjoyable.

29

"We're on the move again, Helen," Pete told his colleague over the encrypted phone.

"Why? What's happened?" she asked hurriedly.

"Had some information about that woman who our friends lost track of after that underground bombing in Holborn. Clocked her organising a couple of blokes loading a removals van. Some furniture but not much. Got the van's reg number and then followed it."

"Not too closely I hope."

"Nah, course not. What d'you take me for?"

Helen didn't say anything.

"But the interesting thing is she now swings between two different addresses … and with two different blokes."

"Two?" she asked. "Where?"

"Rugeley."

"Rugeley?" Helen asked.

"Yep."

"What, Staffordshire?"

"D'you know another one?"

Helen shook her head.

"The old man wants us to keep eyes on. Doesn't want others involved. Not yet. More secure that way."

Helen put the phone down and began to pack some things away.

30

"I heard a strange story about your place in London while you were away."

"Oh, what was it?"

Having recently arrived back in Bristol from her stay in Dublin, Briony was at her brother's place chatting over a cup of coffee about her trip home. He pulled up a chair and sat down at the kitchen table, then sighed.

"You won't be able to go back there. Not now. Not even in the future."

"Why not for fuck's sake?"

Connor sipped his coffee and looked at his sister for a few seconds.

"Apparently your landlord's been telling some of my mates that his workmen had been in your flat to service your boiler and they'd found all sorts of things."

Briony's head turned quickly and she looked at Connor seriously.

"What sort of things?" she demanded curiously.

Connor put his cup down and sat back in his chair.

"My mate said he'd told them they'd found more listening devices and cameras than there are near the Russian embassy."

Briony's face changed.

"What?" she screamed. "Who put them there then?"

"Who do you think?"

"How'd they get in?"

Connor pulled a face. Then Briony's fist smashed the table hard.

"Bastards!"

"What?" he asked.

"I had a letter from the landlord saying that his blokes were visiting the flats to see if any needed re-decorating. Bet that was them."

Connor lifted his cup to his mouth, drained the rest of his coffee, and put the cup down on the table.

"Good bloody job you didn't go back after that bombing then eh?"

Briony nodded, but then, she looked at Connor more seriously.

"What's up now?" he asked.

"Just realised how they must've got in."

One of Connor's eyebrows went up very quickly. Go on, tell me, it was asking.

"Reckon that bloody assistant I took on was a plant. I gave her the security lock's numbers when she took the shop keys back to my place. Bet she gave the place a good look round too."

Connor's mouth fell open.

"Bloody hell, girl. Good job you took my advice and went back home to Dublin for a while then eh?"

He chuckled and pointed at her nose.

"See our old friend Doc McGuire did a good job then? Looks really straight now. How did you like your new passport?"

Briony laughed.

"The photo's not bad, Con, thanks. Had it done after I put my hair back to its original colour. Got to say I've come to like it now as well. Had to add some highlights to it though. Hope you didn't mind."

He laughed.

"You look a totally different person now. Changed your name as well."

She smirked when he mentioned that.

"And my driving licence is from the Republic too. Think I owe you for all this, Con. Thanks."

"Don't thank me, girl. That's what families are for."

She pecked her brother's cheek.

"Don't forget, sis, they had some good photos of you."

"Mmmm. Not any more they don't."

31

The girls in the office where Jack worked were a great bunch to work alongside, easy to get on with, especially one of them, Steph, who had not long been promoted to Accounts Supervisor.

She was married. Twenty-eight years old and blond. Well, sometimes, because other colours appeared whenever she felt like a change. And to Jack that change seemed to happen every two or three days.

Steph was almost five-foot-five, slim, and very good-looking. Had three kids too. Was good at her job. Very reliable and, best of all, she had a contagious smile and wicked sense of humour, which Jack reckoned was a necessity considering all the changes she made to the colour of her hair.

They all got on like a bunch of kids at school. Friendly banter developed through the office and they gave as good as they got. Jack encouraged it. Made for a happy work force.

32

A few miles away from where Jack was living, Brendan's uncle Michael was looking at the old photo of his father that was in a silver frame on the sideboard. Remembered what a brilliant chemist he'd been. How he'd worked for the government in one of its research establishments. How he'd been able to pass on certain bomb-making processes to some of his friends. Remembered all the things his old man had taught him. How he'd encouraged him to go to university all those years ago. *'Work hard on the sciences, lad,'* he'd told him.

Couldn't forget his own graduation either. Two first-class honours degrees from Cambridge. Physics and Chemistry. Remembered all the celebrations they'd had afterwards.

He smiled for a few moments, but then Michael's smile evaporated as he recalled the day his father had been killed.

His boss had sent for him and after asking Michael how his family was, the boss then asked how his dad was. Still wondering what his boss was getting at, Michael simply told him he was fine. He'd visited his mother and father only the week before. It'd been his father's birthday.

His boss hutched about uncomfortably in his chair.

"I'm very sorry to have to inform you, Michael, but your father was killed in an explosion this morning."

He looked up at Michael for a moment.

"Killed?" Michael swore. "What sort of explosion, for God's sake?"

"The police wouldn't tell me anymore, Michael, so you'll have to take that up with them I'm afraid."

There was silence for what seemed hours until his boss told him to go home. Take a couple of weeks off. Compassionate leave with full pay, he insisted. And going home that morning Michael was unable to take in what his boss had just told him.

Days later, having had to live with a friend because of the damage to his home, Michael himself had been thoroughly interviewed by the police. It'd lasted several days, and it was quite nasty too. They believed his father had been killed by a bomb he was making at his home. And they weren't very sorry about it either, because it had all the similarities of other bombs they'd dealt with. Michael was devastated and found it hard to believe. He tried to reason why his father would be so negligent. After all he'd been one of the best. So he'd been told.

There were of course various stories in the media about what had happened, most of them conspiracy theories with bad maths thrown in, making two and two equal five to sell the papers. Some even blamed the gas-board. But Michael came to the conclusion that he'd never really know what had happened.

Devoted as he was to his one-time mentor and to the beliefs he held dear, Michael promised to continue the work his father had so wanted him to do. But instead of following in his father's footsteps he took a sideways step into a different world. Demolition and explosives. Ducks and water. Michael enjoyed making a bang. And the bigger it was the better it was.

Thinking then, how his father had never been shown any recognition for any of the dangerous work he'd done for Queen and country, Michael's thoughts changed. After all, he told himself, it wasn't *his* bloody country.

Hate now flowed through his body.

Dusting the glass on his father's photograph, Michael put it back on the sideboard, then he picked up an envelope that was nearby. He read through a letter that was inside it and looked at the photocopies of a couple of documents his solicitor had sent.

A signature was required.

Michael rang his friend. Told him he'd see him later in the week to sign the documents for the land registry. Thanked him for his work. For his confidentiality and discretion.

But more seriously, for his silence.

33

About half a mile along the canal from Jack's home was a pub. The Bridge. Became his local. Just a ten- or fifteen-minute stroll away, depending how fast he walked. However, Jack had started jogging before going to work. Used the pub as his turn-round point.

At only five-foot-seven and weighing nearly thirteen stone, Jack was trying to get back into shape. Like he used to be. And the injury to his leg wasn't helping. But he enjoyed the morning runs no matter what the weather was or what pain his leg gave him. After a while he thought his local was too near and started running further along the canal to another pub and back. This became his regular six-mile run. Sometimes he ran in the opposite direction until after he ran further, he found he could do circular routes of more than twelve miles. He liked that.

Reminded Jack of how his life used to be.

34

Looking tired but friendly, The Bridge was a good place to socialise. At one end, where he always sat, was a small area that the locals generally used. There were a few tables dotted around that end and a small TV was mounted high up one wall. Nothing special. There were two log fires. One at the local's end, the other in the restaurant area where about twenty tables were situated.

Behind the long, dark, wood-panelled bar which faced you as you walked in were a couple of large mirrors, dividing the shelves that displayed various bottles of spirits. Below them were the fridges containing different bottles of beer, non-alcoholic drinks, cans, and bottles of wine, and at the end of the shelves was a tea-, coffee-, and hot chocolate-making machine. Optics held the most popular spirits and decorating the bar-top were several lagers and beers.

The carpets looked frayed where they'd been joined together some years ago. Probably the originals. There were large hand-written notices above the bar to tell the punters what the pub's next entertainment was and when it was going to take place. Another sign was above the other fireplace and sandwich-boards outside advertised the nights that special meals were being served. Wednesdays, for instance, was Curry Night. Got a free pint with that too.

From one end of the pub to the other was over a hundred feet. A similar area outside at the front was flag-stoned. Several wooden tables with benches and chairs were left there throughout the year. Usually full in the summer especially when it was sunny.

Behind the pub was a large narrow garden that backed onto the canal some twenty feet below. This garden also had its own tables and benches too, but it didn't get the sun. Trees grew from the canal side, sheltering the garden. Faced north though, like Jack's patio.

The four or five staff always met him with smiling faces. They were chatty and cheerful, telling the latest jokes they'd heard over the bar. And there wasn't a quick turn-over of staff that some pubs had which was always a good sign. Their manager, Russ, took the piss out of them when he thought they wouldn't mind. Did it even if they did, but he got the same from them too.

35

It was in this pub one night that Jack noticed a guy he hadn't seen before. Always got a pint and sat with his back to the bar at one of the high round tables in the locals' area facing the TV near the door to the function room. He had a newspaper with him which he spread out across the table. Did the crossword puzzle.

Whenever Jack went in, the man was there with his paper. Only had a couple of pints then he left. Always sat in the same seat though. Like Jack really. And when he got his pint from the bar, they nodded a silent hello, but nothing else. Never said cheerio or anything when he left either. In fact, he never really spoke to anyone.

Jack took a sip of his lager and, relaxing with his pint, his book, and a bag of salted pea-nuts, he found his attention was suddenly drawn to an attractive woman who'd just come in. Hadn't seen *her* there before either. Looked smartly dressed too.

She stood at the bar waiting to be served and after buying a glass of white wine she moved to a table between Jack's and the man with the paper, looked around the place and then sat down facing the bar.

Her straight shoulder-length ginger hair had flecks of bright orange here and there. Reminded him of some of Steph's hairdos that he liked. The woman looked fit too.

She was wearing a tight dark-blue skirt with a matching double-breasted jacket that had two rows of gold buttons down the front. Looked almost like a Navy uniform, but Jack knew it wasn't. She was carrying an expensive-looking plain black handbag that had several lucky charms dangling from one end of the bag's shoulder strap.

They produced a tinkling sound each time the handbag moved. Nothing loud or intrusive. The sorts of things that adorned women's handbags.

When she sat down, she smoothed her skirt out and took her jacket off. Her thin pink blouse didn't leave much to the imagination either. She looked very professional though. Perhaps a director's PA Jack was thinking. *Lucky boss,* he said to himself, and before she sipped some more of her wine, she took a small mirror from out of her handbag. Jack watched, admiring her. And for whatever reason he couldn't understand, she began to liven up the colour on her lips. Looked alright to Jack and the colour matched her blouse too.

After redecorating her lips, she sat quietly drumming her fingers on the table, as though she were waiting for someone, angry that the he or she was late. She seemed anxious though and kept looking round the pub. First Jack's way, then the other. Definitely waiting for someone.

The guy with his crossword was nibbling the end of his pen. His eyebrows knitted together for a few seconds. Perhaps he'd just found the answer to twenty-three down. However, he was still casting his eyes over at the woman, watching her as she kept staring round the room at the other people in the pub. First of all, she looked down to the restaurant area, then at the guy and the others near the bar, before she finally glanced at Jack again.

It looked quite suspicious to him and pretending to look at what was going on at the other end of the pub whilst sipping his pint and reading his book, he began, just out of interest, to watch her as well, appearing innocent of what she was doing.

Every so often she looked at her watch and after twenty minutes or so she finished her wine and left. She *did* nod goodnight to him though. He liked that. But seconds later, the guy folded up his paper and left the pub as well.

Sipping his pint, Jack wondered why the guy had followed her. Perhaps they were secretly meeting somewhere outside. Couldn't have known each other or they'd have sat together. Or would they? Didn't make sense. Perhaps they were having an affair? Then he chuckled to himself. Could be on the game.

It amused him. Made him wonder what they'd do next time they came in. If they did. However, Jack now found himself thinking more about the woman than the man.

There was something familiar about her and he didn't like it.

36

"Good morning Natasha," Sir David said when his PA had shown her into his office. "Please take a seat. Don't worry, you're not in trouble."

Nervously, Natasha McDonald sat down, crossed her legs, and looked across the large mahogany desk at Sir David.

"Coffee?" he asked politely.

"Er, no thank you sir," she replied. "Yvonne and I had one not long ago."

"I know," he replied, nodding his head. "I was sitting nearby."

Pausing to shuffle some papers on his desk, Natasha relaxed a little. It wasn't everyday someone on her pay scale was invited to Sir David's office.

He looked up at his guest.

"I couldn't help overhearing what you were talking about and I wanted to hear your story because it sounded like it had been fun."

Natasha McDonald took a deep breath and relaxed.

"Well," she began, "in the late sixty's my mum went to college near Stafford. Their accommodation was in what had been an old army barracks and was called Nelson Hall. H-blocks they were, and they were a part of Madeley College's campus not far away."

Sir David began to take notes, nodding and scribbling furiously as Natasha waited to carry on with her tale. She paused for him to stop writing and when he had, he looked up, asking her to continue.

"Mum used to tell us stories when we were young, and this always used to frighten us. She told us that when they were on their way back from the pub in Millmeece, just a mile or so away, she and her friends used to hear strange noises coming from one of the fields."

Sir David raised his head, took off his spectacles, and smiled knowingly at her.

"She told us that one night they decided to investigate and went into the field to see what the strange noises were and where they may have been coming from."

Sir David put his spectacles down on the large leather-bound pad of green blotting paper that was on his desk.

"And was your mother successful?" he asked with interest.

"No sir," Natasha sighed. "I'm sorry to say she wasn't. In fact, she said when they got near, the noises terrified them so much they all ran away and never dared to go back and try again."

Sir David's face broke into a broad smile whilst he continued to write, and without looking up at Natasha he thanked her for her time and for relating the story of her mother's frightening experience.

After Natasha McDonald had left Sir David's office, he then asked his PA to put him through to an old friend of his who had been with the Special Reconnaissance Regiment, Major Geoff Shaw, OBE. MC. RM (Ret'd).

37

Summer was coming to an end and the late September evening air had a distinctly cooler feel to it. It must have felt chillier because the guy with his newspaper was now wearing a short thick zip-up fleece. Still did a crossword too.

And when the woman came in, she must have been feeling the change in the weather too, because the clothes she was wearing were of a thicker material and the skirt was much longer. Jack silently approved of the long black boots she had on as well. Reckoned the thin two-inch heels made her look quite sexy.

Despite all that she also looked a little less anxious even though she still drummed her fingers on the table. Habit perhaps. But nothing had changed.

The guy with his paper still sat there, content to finish his crossword and the woman was still silently drumming her fingers on the top of the table whilst she sipped her wine. And when she left the pub the guy always followed seconds later. And that was what Jack found interesting.

He was sure they knew each other, but he couldn't ask. Wasn't any of his business.

Not then. Not there.

A couple of nights later, however, after he'd got his pint, having chatted and exchanged a few jokes with some of the lads at the bar, he wandered over to his usual table in the corner and sat down with his back to the wall. He enjoyed sitting there. Gave him a good view of everyone who came into the pub.

It wasn't long before the guy with his paper came in, got his pint, and sat himself down at the high table as usual. He looked round the pub, opened the paper, took his pen from out of his jacket pocket and started to do the crossword.

Jack was reading a book he'd recently bought from one of the local charity shops. He enjoyed a good read. And resting the book on the table he casually looked up every so often, watching the guy, wondering at the same time just how long it would be before the young woman arrived.

Didn't have to wait long.

In she breezed, got her drink, then, wandering back to the table she liked sitting at each night, she walked straight passed the guy with his crossword, ignoring him completely.

That evening she was wearing jeans with a thick yellow long-sleeved sweater. She'd been carrying her short brown coat and just before she sat down, she hung it neatly over the back of her chair.

Jack was impressed and watched.

Ten minutes later, after getting her make-up from her handbag, she once again began to freshen up her lippy, but this time, as she applied yet more paint, holding the compact mirror in her right hand she slowly moved it further away from her face. Not quite at arm's length, but just far away enough to see Jack's face in it. She hesitated and took a deep breath.

In the small mirror she smiled at Jack's face and winked discreetly at his reflection. He noticed and was amused by what she'd done so he continued to gaze at her. And, being the red-blooded male he was, he eventually winked back as she continued slowly putting the finishing touches to her newly glossed lips.

Agreeing with the end result, Jack nodded his head at her which brought a smile to her face. But at the same time a warning voice in his head was telling him something else.

Good trick, it told him. Seen it before.

But a second later the silent warning had morphed into silliness when he thought she really was on the game and was now trying to pick *him* up.

Her fingers began drumming on the table again. Just three. Triplet rhythm. Da da da, da da da, da da da. Made the old guy suddenly raise his head from out of his crossword and look towards her. He too was watching her fingers tapping away.

Perhaps she was playing some music in her head, beating out the rhythm to it, Jack didn't know, but as soon as she'd started, the guy stopped doing his crossword and stared at her for a minute. Then, picking up his pen he wrote something on the side of the page of his newspaper.

Jack was more intrigued now and wanting another pint he got up to get another one. But just after he'd picked his pint up off the bar, he was suddenly surround by lots of people. He pushed his way through them and sat back down in the corner. More people were piling in. Some getting a pint or two on their way home from work whilst others moved into the restaurant area to have a meal out.

38

Listening to the phone ringing relentlessly the caller was about to let it ring for just another couple of times, but he couldn't stand the noise and decided not to. Realised Jack must be out.

He had something to tell him and it was very important. He thought about leaving a message on Jack's answer-machine, but he didn't. Thought better of it. He wasn't sure if the number he was calling was really Jack's and he didn't want to get *that* wrong. People might become suspicious.

Daring not to risk it, he decided he'd have to meet Jack face to face somewhere. Have to get a message to him when he had time on his hands. And that wasn't going to be very soon.

The man put his phone down, picked up his small bag that was always packed with a few things he needed, and left the house.

39

It was only when a large group of twenty-year-olds flooded the place that things began to happen in the pub and while two of the lads stood at the bar to get their drinks, the others pushed between the woman's table and those nearby, knocking into them and spilling some of the locals' drinks. It became more evident that the word 'apologise' wasn't in their dictionary.

They pushed some tables together, moved the chairs and generally began pissing the locals off by barging into them like they owned the place. They redesigned the local's area, talked loudly about nothing in particular, which made Russ stand at the end of the bar to keep an eye on them all just in case things kicked off.

A loud cheer went up from the noisy group when the two guys joined it with their drinks and a few seconds later a party began.

Surrounded by all the noise, the woman was now looking somewhat distressed. She turned to face Jack. She looked as though she was hoping he'd somehow rescue her. But he didn't. He just kept watching, still trying to think who she was. He was interested at the way things were now developing. Even the bloke with his crossword was too.

Ten minutes later, the woman was frowning, looking angrily at her so-called neighbours as though she could have killed them all. She definitely wanted to be somewhere else. After all, she was in the middle of the rumpus and didn't like it.

Fidgeting about, uncomfortable sitting there, she lifted the glass to her lips and began to gulp her wine.

Very quickly.

40

As more people came into the pub that evening the young woman looked more and more stressed because she was in the midst of the noise.

She suddenly turned and faced Jack.

"Excuse me," she shouted in a stage whisper that was louder than the commotion. "Would you mind if I joined you?"

That took Jack by surprise. Women didn't ask him that sort of thing. He stared at her. Saw her pleading smile shouting for help.

"Be my guest," he replied nervously, having seen the predicament she was in. And jumping up he pulled a chair out for her, hoping her husband, if she had one, wasn't going to come in just then and spoil the fun.

As she collected her coat and handbag, she picked up her glass. Jack's friends at the bar were now laughing, cheering, and putting their thumbs up at him.

Pulled!

The young woman plonked her handbag on the floor next to her feet, hung her coat over her chair, and sat down facing Jack.

He liked her in the yellow sweater, but as lovely as it looked, he preferred the pink blouse she'd worn the first time he'd seen her.

She took a deep breath, sighed deeply, then sipped more of her wine. This seemed to relax her.

You men are so easy, she mused as the wine trickled down her throat. She looked across at Jack.

"Sorry about that," she smiled apologetically. "Heard that lot making rude comments about my clothes and I can't stand that sort of thing. Also hate it when people get too near me. Makes me feel trapped."

Jack listened as she looked over her shoulder for a second or two at the noisy crowd.

"Know what you mean. Suffer from it too," he lied. "Claustrophobia, isn't it?"

She smiled at him, looking happier that he'd understood how she felt.

"Hope you don't mind. Still getting my bearings," she began. "Not been here long."

Jack listened as he sipped his pint. Couldn't place her accent, but he realised he knew her voice and the thought of Val came to mind and put him on edge. But he thought it was also the voice of Briony and *that* made the hair on his neck stand up. However, before he could dwell on it, she held her hand out.

"Sorry," she said shyly, "I'm Rachel."

"Pleased to meet you," he told her, lying through his teeth. "I'm Jack."

And he put his thoughts of Briony to one side. For the time being.

Rachel stifled an embarrassing laugh and Jack looked at the gold ring on her finger then looked at her.

"Boyfriend not joining you tonight then?" he asked cautiously.

She spread the fingers of her hand out wide and looked at the ring.

"Not tonight," she replied casually, without a care in the world. "He's had to work."

The conversation went quiet for a while then she asked, "D'you work round here?"

He nodded and told her he was the accounts manager for a

private transport company a few miles from there.

She looked very interested when he told her.

"Oh, what's it called?" she asked enthusiastically.

"Roger's Transport," he told her.

She appeared to have heard of it.

"And do you work round here as well?" he asked her.

She nodded as she finished her wine.

"Sainsburys in Stafford," she told him. "I'm the HR manager there."

She sniggered, adding that some of the staff nick-named her The Laughin' Assassin.

It made Jack chuckle, thinking about some of those he knew who'd been like that and then, more seriously, he remembered those he knew who did it for a living.

Rachel looked very surprised when he picked her empty glass up, took it to the bar and bought her another drink. When he returned, she gave him another beautiful smile, which made Jack feel suddenly wary. Hadn't felt like that for some time and it wasn't because she was smiling at him or that she was engaged. Jack was seriously wondering how big her partner might be, and here she was, teasing him, letting her fingers playfully move up and down the stem of her wine glass, flirting with it. Flirting with him.

She smiled to herself and looked down at the engagement ring on her finger again whilst Jack was looking across at the guy with his paper. He was now chewing the inside of his cheek and looked deep in thought about something. Sixteen across?

He was staring at Jack though, and not just staring but glaring at him. Not just at him either, but right through him.

Jack glanced at the guy and although he thought he was probably just thinking about another word to write in the crossword, he was becoming aware of just how much the guy had really been watching them both. And the more he thought about it, the more the name O'Shea began to appear in his mind.

Are you one of them? he wondered.

However, Rachel brought him back to the real world when she started to chat about how nice the town was to live in; how pleasant the people were; how unusual it was to have two supermarkets in such a small town. Then, she remarked how safe a place it was to live.

Jack hadn't given it much thought until that moment and agreeing with her he nodded his head. It was. But the word 'safe' had made the hair on the back of his neck stand up again, bringing back the name that just moments ago had also resurfaced. *Why safe?* he pondered. *Two questions now.* And there were two people as well.

Are you both O'Shea's?

41

In his newly rented office, Pete picked up the secure phone and dialled a number. He waited for someone to pick it up at the other end and was just about to take another bite of his half-eaten sausage sandwich when a voice answered.

"Hi Pete."

"Bloody hell, boss, you must be psychic or do you know the sound of my phone now?"

He heard her laughing.

"Stupid bugger. Your name comes up on the screen."

He chuckled.

"So what's up?" she asked.

Pete put his half-eaten sandwich back down on his desk.

"Got a new guy on the scene now," he said excitedly.

"Eh? When?"

"Beginning of the week. Our target initiated the friendship as well. Very clever the way she did it too. Used her mirror when she put her lippy on and caught his eye. She winked. He winked back. And hey presto! *Houston, we have a problem,*" he joked. "Haven't seen that one for ages. It's an old trick, but it still works. She sits with him every time she goes in the pub now as well."

"Mmmm, interesting. Thanks Pete."

42

"Is that right, Con's sister's taken her gran's name now then?" Sean asked quietly from across the table.

He was visiting Brendan in prison so they kept the conversation light in case they made the prison officers suspicious. Brendan looked at his friend and nodded.

"Mmmm," he agreed. "He suggested it just after that trouble in London. He's not as daft as people think."

Sean nodded, letting his eyes rove round the room just in case any of the warders were getting too near. Might hear something they shouldn't and report it later to someone higher up. Couldn't trust them.

"Yeah. Had to really though, didn't she?"

Sean nodded, keeping a vigilant eye on those in the room.

"Mr McGuire gave her a new nose by all accounts," he whispered from the other side of the table. "She arrived back in the UK with a different passport that has a few stamps in it, and they gave her a proper driver's licence too."

Sean sniggered quietly, knowing exactly what he meant.

"Dec's already up there helping Michael, thank God. She went up later though with that so-called fuckin' partner of hers cos he got a new job. They're still not getting on though. Don't know why she's put up with him for so long. Heard he's still up to his old tricks as well. Just hope he keeps his bloody mouth shut, eh?"

They both laughed, then Brendan continued.

"She really does hate him, Sean, but not half as much as the guy who put me in here though. She told me if ever she meets him again, she's going to take him out."

And nodding his head Sean knew it wouldn't be on a date.

43

By mid-November Jack was now jogging along the canal every morning before breakfast, overtaking some runners and passing those who were jogging the other way, but none of them seemed to say much. One or two said or nodded a quick and breathless 'hi' which reminded him of his days when he'd been hiking in the mountains around Europe. Weren't like the runners. The walkers over there always had time to say hello when you met them, whoever you were.

During his runs along the canal a young woman jogging with one of these groups had caught Jack's eye. Looked younger than him. Wasn't always with the group either, but she always said hello. Looked very fit too, in every sense of the word, and Jack hoped she wasn't attached to any of her running friends.

A few days later he found out.

"Phew," she gasped, having caught up with him on his way back home. "You're setting a good pace this morning, aren't you?" she asked as a bit of friendly banter. "Getting your leg back into shape then?"

They slowed down to a fast walk, causing the heat from their bodies to produce small clouds of mist that floated away and disappeared the same way your breath does on a cold morning.

"Trying to get everything back into shape," he laughed.

"Good for you. Must've been a very bad accident to get an injury like that."

Jack nodded his head, muttering between breaths that it had been, but that it was all in the past now. The woman pulled a face and gave him a smile that said 'oh' as if she clearly wanted to know more about it. He realised then that he hadn't heard her behind him and tried to think where she could have joined the canal path. She certainly wasn't on it when he'd turned round to go back home.

"D'you do this every morning then?" she asked.

"Just about," he told her. "Sometimes I go the other way, why? You want to join me?"

They picked up speed and began to jog again, not at a fast pace, just a comfortable one.

"Well, presuming you do this at the same time, I'd like that if you don't mind. The guys I've been running with slow me down too much, if you know what I mean?"

Jack nodded his head and looked at her.

She was about his height and had very short dark hair. She was wearing some pink tracky-bottoms and a thin long-sleeved matching top. Looked so fit he wondered what she did.

"Well, I usually get onto the path about six," he explained. "By that bridge near Tesco."

"Mmmm, sounds OK. You sure you don't mind me joining you though?" she asked. "I know some people like to run on their own."

Her smile would have melted the ice at the North Pole, if it could have seen her, but it didn't so the ice remained in place and Jack began to think about her running with him. Could be interesting company to say the least.

"If you're not there at six, I won't wait," he told her, emphasising the point to let her know he was a stickler for punctuality.

She looked across at him and shook her head.

"Don't worry, I'll be there," she snapped. "Would hate to keep you waiting."

They laughed and although her comment was slightly sarcastic, Jack reckoned she knew he really meant it.

"Oh," she said suddenly, "I'm Michelle. New round here. Just moved up from Bristol. How d'y'do?"

As they jogged along the canal path, they shook hands with each other and he noticed something wrong with the little finger of her left hand. The top joint was missing completely which made him wonder how she'd done it, but then he saw there were no rings on her fingers. And that really pleased him.

"And I'm Jack," he said, and tried to place her accent.

A mile further along the canal, he told Michelle that he was leaving her. Her face shouted 'what?'

"My stop," he told her. "Only live about a hundred yards away."

She looked surprised, said cheerio to him, adding that she'd be there tomorrow promptly at six and waved as she ran further along the canal path.

44

Having done a lot of homework, the man who had mugged the photographer in Bristol had eventually learned that Jack was now living in Rugeley, but he wasn't sure the address he'd been given was correct. From what he'd been given though, with help from some of his other friends, he'd also been able to trace Jack's landline number. Still couldn't use it. Wouldn't have been a wise thing to do. He knew Jack's phone wouldn't be secure. Not for what he wanted to talk about.

He felt angry at not being able to contact him though. Felt frustrated by the things he was no longer sure of. Didn't know how Jack was feeling now. It'd been a while since he'd seen him, and he was getting desperate to meet and talk to him.

And desperate needs meant desperate actions.

45

"Dad?" the young lad began to ask.

His father raised his head from the newspaper.

"What's up, lad?"

He put the paper down on the table and looked at his son.

"Well," he began again. "Bill and I were playing in one of Charlie Anderson's fields the other day, but it started raining so we ran into that ditch between the two rows of trees to get out of the rain."

His Dad expected to hear another story from his imaginative, adventurous seven-year old.

"And what happened?" he asked, wondering what story he was going to hear this time. "Was the place swarming with pirates waiting to kidnap you and take you off to sea?"

His son sniggered.

"Don't be silly, Dad," he said, as if telling him off.

And Dad chuckled.

"So what did you do then?"

The lad moved to the table and sat down next to his Dad.

"We found some tubes sticking out of the ground."

His father picked up his cup and sipped some of his tea.

"Tubes eh?"

Josh looked at his father, nodded and frowned.

"There was a noise coming from them though, Dad."

His father frowned then, showing more interest in his son's ramblings.

"What sort of noise, Josh?"

"Don't know really," he began. "It was sort of a machinery sound, but it frightened us, so we ran away."

Police Constable Cookson wasn't shocked. His son was always coming home with stories like that whenever he'd been out playing in the fields near their home. Reminded him of some of the Rupert the Bear stories that he'd read himself as a kid.

And while PC Cookson continued to read his paper, believing what his son had just told him was nothing more than playful imagination, his son ran off to see his friend Bill who had reappeared at the back door to see if he was coming out to play again.

46

At 6 a.m., when Jack approached the canal path for his early morning run, Michelle was already there. Loosening up. Waiting. She was wearing her pink tracky-bottoms and a thin vest under her fleece which was undone. Jack stopped to look at her for a few seconds, smiling to himself. Michelle was running on the spot and each time one of her feet touched the path her small breasts danced freely inside her vest. It amused him.

She was tapping her fingers on the face of her watch as well. Irritated. Wasn't pleased.

"Late," she snapped angrily when he was close enough to hear her.

Jack shrugged his shoulders. And?

"Y'watch must be fast then," he returned.

He was about to laugh, but Michelle wasn't in the mood.

"What is it about you guys? Arrange a time then y'don't bloody well turn up! Good job we're not catching a plane!"

Jack said sorry, then reminded her that Rugeley didn't have an airport, leaving Michelle resigned to the fact that he really wasn't that bothered.

They ran off down the path with Jack setting the pace. Not too fast though. He was thinking about his co-runner. Well he was, until she asked why he was going so slowly. Had to up his game then. And she kept up with him too.

By the time they reached the half-way point Jack was amazed that Michelle wasn't even out of breath and he found himself lagging behind.

Laughing at him, she turned and told him to keep up. Embarrassed him. Challenged his male ego. Made him wonder then what she did.

"So where d'you work then?" he managed to ask between breaths.

By then they were side by side after Michelle had slowed down enough for Jack to catch up with her.

"I'm with the Rail Network. Plan the entire region's track-maintenance. Have to inspect it when it's completed too."

"Wow! Enjoy it then?" he asked.

Michelle nodded.

"Yes. Suppose I do. The hours are sometimes weird, but whose aren't these days?"

She turned her head towards him.

"That why you don't always run in the mornings then?" Jack asked.

She nodded, realising he'd evidently noticed her absence some mornings and made a mental note to not run every day. Well, not where *he* would see her.

When Jack left the canal path Michelle stayed with him until he went into his house. Without stopping she smiled to herself, knowing exactly where he lived, and ran across the road towards Morrisons' car park.

47

Parked up near Morrisons early that wet morning a man sat in the comfort of his car. Alone. Hoping and waiting to see if his old friend really did live at the address he'd been given.

He watched Jack return from his morning jog, soaked to the skin. It made the man chuckle to himself.

Before the man in his car had seen Jack return, he'd also watched quite a few other joggers running along the road from the canal bridge, and, looking at Jack's house beyond the rain splashing on his windscreen, he waited patiently. It was something he was extremely good at.

He looked and saw a solitary jogger running across the road towards the car park just a few minutes after Jack had gone into his house. On reaching Morrisons' car park the solitary runner appeared to slow down a little before continuing past the man's car. Whether or not the nod of the runner's head was caused by the jogging movement, no one would have known. But the man did. So too did the runner. And the man knew then that the information he'd been given was correct.

As he sat there waiting he unwrapped a Mars Bar and bit into it. They weren't anywhere near as large as they used to be, he recalled. Softer too. His thoughts were interrupted when he saw Jack drive off to work.

And a few minutes later the man started his car and went to work as well.

48

That Thursday evening Jack rushed home from work, showered, put on some aftershave, and got changed to go out. Normally, he'd have popped to the pub, but this wasn't normal. Rachel had asked him if they could walk to the pub along the canal and he'd agreed. But only because he really wanted to find out as much as he could about her.

Going to the kitchen window, he kept looking through it in case she was anywhere to be seen and minutes later he watched a car suddenly pull up in the large open space that was there for people to use when visiting those who lived in that particular row of terraced houses.

Rachel got out.

"Lucky partner," he said to the curtains as he peered through the kitchen window.

She looked lost, wondered where Jack was. She turned towards his house and he waved. Made a funny face at her from the window. But she saw him, and, baring her teeth, she pretended to snarl at him. Then, she stuck her tongue out and laughed.

They met at the front door and standing back a little, she looked at the row of old terraced houses, peering through Jack's open front door trying to see what his place was like inside. As if she'd like to be shown around.

"Didn't know you lived here, Jack," she said as she pecked him on his cheek.

"Never asked, Raich," he said.

She looked gone out at being called Raich and stifled a giggle. But she liked it. That was first time anyone had used a shortened version of her name and Jack noticed.

"So are we walking along the tow path then?"

Jack looked down to see what she'd got on her feet to make sure she'd be OK. He felt relieved. She wasn't in her sling-backs. He nodded.

"It's just across the bridge," he told her, pointing the way.

She frowned. Didn't look too happy about it, even though it had been her suggestion, and it was getting dark too.

"There aren't any weirdos along there if that's what you're worried about. It's perfectly safe, Raich."

Then he realised he'd just said the word 'safe' and he began to feel uneasy about going that way. OK there were streetlights along the path, but what if there were some weirdos? O'Shea's weirdos?

What if?

He felt Rachel gripping his hand and the 'ifs' disappeared.

"And how long will it take us?" she asked slowly, looking up into the sky wondering if it was going to rain again.

"Oh about fifteen minutes or so," he told her.

Unconvinced with his answer, she looked at her watch.

"Better get a move on then in case we get lost on the way and the pub's closed," she joked.

She let go of Jack's hand, linked her arm through his, and together they walked round the end of the terraced houses, over the bridge and down the slope to the canal path.

Jack felt happy walking with Rachel that evening, even though he was still unsure about her and despite her joking that she'd push him in the canal if he tried anything, she clung on to him hard, thrilled when he'd picked her up and carried her over a few large puddles along the way. She'd laughed when Jack had almost dropped her in one when he'd struggled to lift her up, but he'd wanted her to think he wasn't very strong and it had worked.

"God man," she said, telling him off. "You want to get down the gym and build some muscles up, mate."

He laughed and, having not met any weirdos along the way, they arrived at the pub without any mishaps.

Rachel looked at her watch again.

"Mmmm," she murmured as they went in, "you were right. Fifteen minutes precisely."

Inside, Jack ordered their drinks and they sat at their usual table, facing each other. He saw the guy with his newspaper come in, get his pint, and sit facing their way from his lofty viewpoint. The guy nodded in their direction, but when Jack nodded back, he got a dubious shake of the head in return, as if he knew something about them that Jack didn't. The guy began writing something on the page again. But what puzzled Jack even more was that he seemed to have been doing that quite a lot recently.

49

Two days before meeting Jack, along a different street, in a different house, just a few miles away, Rachel was finishing her breakfast. And standing next to her at the kitchen table was Declan. With his mousy unkempt hair falling over his eyes he looked a bit younger than her, but he wasn't, and he was angry.

His feet were planted firmly apart. His arms hung loosely down by his sides and he was staring hard at Rachel.

He suddenly thumped his fist on the table, making everything on it shake.

"And where the fuck did you get to last night?" he growled.

Unfazed by Declan's outburst, Rachel yawned slowly, stretched her arms and fingers out wide, and then, rubbing the bed out of her eyes, she blinked.

Four times.

"And what the fuck's it got to do with you?" she asked in disgust.

If looks could kill, she'd have died there and then. But looks don't kill. Never have. And watching the guy's hands for any other signs of movement, the fingers of Rachel's left hand walked their way stealthily across the table to her open handbag and gripped the Walther PPK that she kept hidden there.

Declan didn't move.

He'd seen how one of her fingers was curled round the trigger. He also knew she wouldn't hesitate to use the weapon if she had to. Even on him. She was like that.

"Look!" he shouted. "I don't know why you want to find that

bloke, but if you keep going out and getting pissed you won't, will you?"

She sneered at him and stood up.

"Hey! When I go out, I don't get pissed!" she screamed.

And as each word shot out of her mouth, she prodded him in the chest with one finger.

"I. Keep. An. Eye. Out. In. Case. He. Turns. Up. Somewhere. OK?"

"Don't know why you can't forget about him. He's no danger to us, is he?"

Rachel's lips curled up.

"No, he isn't to you," she shouted. "But he put Brendan in prison. And that's enough for me!"

Declan picked up his bag with his flask and sarnies in it and flung it over one shoulder. He sighed. The anger subsided.

"I'm going then," he told her, "but if I find you've been with someone, I'll—"

"You'll fuckin' what?" she interrupted him. "You haven't got the balls!"

Rachel heard him go out of the front door, slamming it shut, rattling the three loose panes of glass that were in it.

"Arsehole!" she shouted down the hall when she heard the noise he'd made.

She finished her breakfast and went upstairs to take a bath.

The bubbles were up to her neck after she lay down in them and after a while she began to think more of what Declan had said about forgetting the bloke, then, she began to think about Jack. She knew he liked her and he wasn't married either. Might be useful.

Her mobile suddenly rang and she cursed at having to answer it, after all, she was a woman having a bath and *that* should never be interrupted, however, from the name on the phone's display, she knew she should answer it.

She put the mobile to her soapy left ear. It was Connor, but during the conversation he just happened to mention that the bloke she was looking for knew how to look after himself in a fight. He then went on to explain all about it and how both he and Pat had literally taken a hell of a beating from him. He told her he must have been highly trained because he'd fought like a one-man army and that could be dangerous.

50

"D'you reckon he ever finishes it, Raich?" he asked as they sat down together.

There were looks of surprise.

"Who? What?"

Jack pointed him out to her and told her about how he looked as though he was always doing a crossword.

"Never noticed, Jack," she replied, leaning towards him, looking at his face. "I've more important things on my mind at the moment."

"Oh, I just thought you two knew each other," he said, pushing for answers.

She frowned.

"Why?" she asked, trying not to look too concerned. "What gave you that impression?"

So Jack told her about her drumming her fingers on the table and how the guy always followed her out of the pub when she left. It made her laugh, but Jack noticed the uncertainty flash across her face.

"Reckon you've been reading too many books, Jack," she commented and took a sip of her wine, but as she did, she turned and quickly glanced back at the guy.

Jack watched and wondered if she really *did* know him, because when she turned back to face him, she didn't look pleased. In fact, she looked quite alarmed.

They continued drinking and chatting about everyday things, trying hard not to bring politics into their conversation.

"Fancy something to eat then, Raich?" he suddenly asked.

She tilted her head. A question was about to be launched his way.

"So what did the last one have then, Jack?" she enquired.

He smirked.

"Eh?"

"Oh c'mon, Jack," she said, teasing him. "Surely y'can't tell me I'm the first woman you've ever brought here for a meal?"

She watched the grin grow across his face. He shook his head. Must have believed him because she leaned right across the table and kissed him on his right cheek. Not a peck though. It lasted a bit longer than that which made him wonder why.

At the bar the lads saw her kissing Jack and began to stick their thumbs up at him. He told her and she giggled. Then, turning towards them, she very bravely blew each one of them a kiss of their own.

Sweet.

Well, it was until Jack looked across at the guy with his paper. The sweetness had then somehow turned sour. And he didn't know why.

Rachel seemed over the moon when Jack placed the bottle of white wine on the table and filled her glass.

"Thank you, Jack," she whispered. "Think you're beginning to spoil me."

The meals arrived and the night continued being a very enjoyable one. Felt romantic too. Hadn't happened for quite some time and Jack wanted it to last a bit longer, but after the meal Rachel began to fidget. Kept looking at her watch.

"Think we ought to make our way back, don't you?" she suggested, moving closer to him as she leaned across the table.

Somewhat disappointed, he agreed. Thought she probably had to get back home in case her partner was wondering where she was or who she was with. Needed to know because Jack had a profound fear of husbands and partners, no matter which woman they belonged to.

"Can we still go back the same way though please?"

She'd evidently noticed the streetlamps all along the canal path when they'd walked to the pub. Jack said it'd be OK and, getting up, he held her short coat out for her. She let him lay it across her shoulders then they made their way out.

They said goodnight to Russ as they passed the bar, but once outside, Rachel turned to face Jack and placing one hand on each side of his face she gently stroked it before cupping it and giving him a long soft kiss.

And due to the many other kisses they gave each other on the way home, it took them longer than fifteen-minutes-precisely to get back, however, once they were, she suddenly told him she'd get a taxi and collect her car in the morning.

His idea of inviting her in was immediately dashed into millions of pieces. He knew the man in her life wouldn't have liked her staying for a drink, but *he* would have.

But she was adamant about getting home, even after all the kisses she'd given him, and he couldn't understand why. He wondered what game she was playing; thought he was being taken for a ride by this seemingly fearless femme fatale.

She kissed him, then took her mobile out of her handbag and phoned for a taxi. Another kiss later.

"You in tomorrow?" she asked before getting in the taxi.

51

"So who was the old bag you were with last night then, Jack? Your gran?"

The girls in the office started giggling.

"Morning Steph," he said as he walked through the outer office to his own, trying hard not to be drawn in by Steph's comments.

She followed him in and plonked his special mug down on his desk. It was one he'd bought when he'd been on holiday hill-walking in Scotland. Jack's favourite place. The mug had the word TORRIDON written all over it in different coloured lettering.

Having pulled up a chair to sit herself down next to him, she made a meal out of making sure her knees were nowhere near his.

"C'mon then, who was she?"

Steph sounded very concerned and Jack suspected she only wanted to know so she could gossip about it.

"Not jealous are you, Steph?" he came back.

From the look he got, he could almost feel the lethal red dot in the centre of his forehead.

"No," she mumbled sharply, "just wondered who she was."

"Where were *you* then?" he asked her.

She screwed her eyes up and looked at him sternly, just like his Mum did whenever he'd done something wrong.

"Driving past your place with m'kids. Just been to junior karate class. You were walking from your place to the canal bridge."

There was a short pause.

"Arm in arm with her as well," she tutted in disgust.

Jack smirked and lifted his mug to his mouth.

"So who was she for fuck's sake?" she asked, raising her voice more this time, but Jack put his mug down and sat back in his chair, smiling, teasing her.

"Come on then, Jack, don't mess about!"

He waited another minute or so, leaned forward, picked up a pencil from his desk and began fiddling with it.

"OK, I'm not speaking to you if you're going to be like this," she said angrily and was about to get up when Jack finally gave in to her demands.

"Met her in the pub some weeks ago."

Steph's head spun round. She looked shocked. "Her name's Rachel. And she's spoken for."

Steph's eyes and mouth opened at the same time.

"Yes Steph. Got a bloke."

"Huh! Suppose I'll have to look a bit more glam now then eh?"

"How d'you mean?"

"Well just look at me," she moaned. "Don't have a bloody chance if you're going to take women like her out, do I?"

She pulled a face.

"Never knew you wanted me to, Steph."

Startled, she looked at him, wondering then, if he might ask her.

"You're just as attractive as she is," he said at last. "And you've a bloke too."

"Mmm, yeah, just not as bloody glamorous though eh?"

And as she walked through the door she started to giggle.

A little later she returned with a few files under her arm, threw them down on Jack's desk, pulled up a chair, and sat down.

"Now what?"

"Reckon I saw her the other day. Strange it was too."

Jack asked her to go on.

"Well, the kids and I were in The Miners having something to eat and she was there with a guy. Tall bloke. About her age. Thought it was one of our drivers at first, but it wasn't. This one looked rough."

She frowned and looked as though she was remembering the scene.

"Probably her bloke, Steph."

"Mmm, well, they met a couple of other blokes too."

Jack's eyebrows rose up.

"And? Aren't people allowed to meet friends any more now then?" he asked sarcastically.

Steph threw an irritable glance in his direction.

"Well, they sat at a table near us. We were by the windows overlooking the car park. She and her bloke were chatting and when the other two came in they all moved outside."

Jack listened.

"Then what happened?" he asked.

"Your friend looked round, took a small bulky package from her shopping bag and handed it to the one of the other blokes. It was like a large padded envelope, but it looked heavy. Didn't see what it was though, well, not just then."

Jack sat back, wondering what was coming next.

"How d'you mean?"

Steph took a breath.

"As he looked inside it, he dropped the bloody thing on the ground. Should've seen their faces. They almost shit themselves. You'd have thought a grenade had just landed at their feet."

"What was it?"

"A gun fell out of the envelope, Jack. Like one of those you see cops using on TV."

Jack frowned and listened as Steph continued.

"The bloke suddenly picked the gun up off the ground and, looking round to see if anyone had seen him, he stuck it back in the envelope out of sight."

"What? Just like that? In the car park?"

"Mmmm," she nodded, "but ..."

Jack waited as Steph took another breath.

"Your friend suddenly grabbed the guy's free hand," she continued, her words speeding up with excitement. "Twisted it and bent it back, ever so hard. Quick as a flash. Nasty too. Thought she was going to break his bloody wrist. Should've seen his face. He was almost on his toes. She pulled him right into her. Very close. Nose to nose like. Must've really hurt him. Looked like she was giving him a really good bollocking. Then she let go of his hand. Y'could see it'd really hurt him though."

She paused for a second.

"He pushed the bag back inside his coat ever so fast."

Jack meanwhile was trying to picture the incident.

"Mmmm. Wouldn't think it was a gun, Steph. It's not a thing you'd let others see. Especially in a car park. You probably saw something else," he told her.

"OK Jack," she conceded, "but I know what I saw, and it looked bloody dodgy to me. And she looked a real nasty bitch too."

Steph stood up, collected Jack's empty coffee mug from his desk, and walked out.

52

Having seen Jack go to work the man in his car turned left out of the car park, following the main road round the mini-roundabout and parked up in a nearby cul-de-sac. On double yellow lines.

Once out of the car, he pulled the hood of his waterproof jacket up over his head, took a paper-boy's fluorescent orange bag from the passenger seat, hauled it over one shoulder and hutching his head down into his shoulders like he didn't enjoy being in the rain he walked back along the road before turning left into Bryans Lane.

He stopped to look at his watch. It was just after nine-fifteen. It was still raining too.

A few yards further along the road he crossed the open space in front of Jack's house and took several pieces of paper from his bag. He shook the rain off his sleeve, looked at the number on Jack's front door and without a care in the world he pushed a handful of circulars through Jack's letterbox.

But it wasn't just Jack's letterbox that he pushed the pieces of paper through. He casually strolled along the entire row of terraced-houses pushing other circulars through each letterbox before returning to his car and driving away.

Job done.

He was wet through. It had been another wet job, but it didn't matter. This one had been a doddle and he knew it hadn't been anywhere near as dangerous as the wet-work he was usually asked to do.

53

Greg's mobile was ringing. It was quite late, but he hoped it was the number he was expecting and he picked the phone up.

"Took your bloody time," he moaned after hearing Jack's voice.

"Yeah, sorry mate," came his reply. "Had to find a phone box that worked. So, what's with the code on the circular then?"

"Never thought you of all people would have forgotten that."

Jack was quiet for a moment or two, thinking.

"Course I remember," he admitted. "Used it in an emergency, didn't we?"

"At fuckin' last. Well done."

"Sorry. Been a long time," he said. "So where and when then, mate?"

"I'll contact you later OK?"

"Like before?" he chuckled.

"Similar."

The call ended and Jack plonked the phone into its holder fast. He had to get out. The phone box stunk of pee and because Jack's phone wasn't secure enough, he'd had no choice but to use that one.

He and Greg needed somewhere they could speak and that certainly wasn't going to be *his* place.

54

Around ten-fifteen that Tuesday night the rain had finally stopped and in the blue Nissan Micra that was parked just off the road, blocking an entrance to a field, a couple sat there talking to each other. Had anyone seen them it would have looked like they were taking some time to themselves, having an affair perhaps whilst enjoying what comes naturally to a loved-up couple as they chatted and kissed each other every so-often.

But these two people weren't loved-up. Nor were they having an affair. Not in a million years. They were simply biding their time until the traffic along the road had quietened down. Something to do until it was time to move.

"The only info I have is that there may be something unusual going on around here and whatever it is we've got to find where it might be. Shouldn't be very far away either."

Greg frowned.

"Where'd that info come from then?"

Cassie smiled.

"One of the girls in the tapping department was chatting about her mum going to college near here and C heard the conversation so when he delved deeper and interviewed her, she told him about the strange noises her mum had told her about years ago. So, you're as knowledgeable about it as I am, Greg."

"Looks like we'll just have to get out and scout around a bit then eh?"

Cassie turned in her seat to undo her seatbelt.

"Well it'll be a bloody start," she said. "At least it's stopped raining."

Greg sighed and nodded in agreement.

"C'mon then mister, let's move into this field and start searching along that thick hedgerow over there."

"Why there?" Greg asked.

"Looks as good a place as any."

They got out of the car and climbed over the broken gate that they'd parked next to.

In the field Cassie switched her pencil torch on and a small beam of light flickered across the wet grass. They walked slowly away from their car, looking into the hedge and every so often Greg turned around to make sure no one was following them. There shouldn't have been, but in their line of work he knew they could never be sure.

He didn't feel happy either. He wasn't armed.

Following the hedgerow downhill about a hundred yards Cassie suddenly stopped. The tall haw-thorn hedgerow changed and became thicker, but it wasn't just one hedge. There were two, concealing a shallow scooped-out ditch, about ten feet wide and some four feet deep. It ran between the two lines of the hedges, hiding anyone or anything from sight. From the field it would have been impossible to see the ditch. Unless you knew it was there.

Even though it'd been raining most of the day the only water in the ditch was off the dripping leaves from the hedgerows above their heads. The ditch hadn't seen water for many a year and as Cassie pointed her torch along it, strange looking things sticking out of the ground some distance away were caught in the beam of light.

Greg and Cassie moved cautiously towards what looked like the ends of a row of old drainpipes.

There were a dozen of them, spaced out about three yards apart.

They looked a bit larger than the average drainpipe though. Probably about six inches in diameter and standing a couple of feet tall.

A few inches above each pipe, however, and attached by some old rusty wire was a cone-shaped top giving the impression that the pipes could be some kind of flues or air vents.

"What the bloody hell are they?" Greg asked.

"Dunno mate," she said. "Not seen anything like it."

They scrambled along the ditch to have a better look.

When they reached the first one, they just stood and looked at it. To begin with they thought the flue was made of UPVC, but on closer examination they found it to be made of thick asbestos. Old stuff. There was also the sound of a low-pitched hum coming from it as well. As if a motor was turning over quietly somewhere below them.

Cassie bent down and put one of her hands on the top of the flue. It was warm and she could feel its slight vibration. Warm air was coming from it too. Extractors, she thought, then she sniffed the pipe, but the smell was of nothing in particular. Just damp earth and warm air.

She looked up at her colleague.

"What d'you reckon then?"

Greg just stood there, shaking his head in disbelief.

They walked on slowly, examining them each in turn. They were all the same. The flues were fixed into the ground by broad rusty metal rings held in place by four large steel nuts set in blocks of concrete that appeared to go quite a way into the ground. Clearly man-made. But what was below them left them clueless and was raising many queries that had to be solved.

After spending nearly an hour looking at the pipes and taking photos of them on Cassie's mobile, she suggested they went back to their car and let those in charge see what they'd found.

55

"What's up son?"

PC Cookson was just getting ready to go to work. He was on the night shift.

"Y'know I told you about those pipe-things up in the fields?"

His Dad nodded his head and fastened the buttons up his coat.

"Well, they weren't there the other day."

PC Cookson frowned. Perhaps his son hadn't been making it up after all.

"How d'you mean, young feller-m'-lad?"

Josh thought for a moment, wondering how he'd describe the scene.

"There was nothing there. The ground looked just like the rest of the ditch."

PC Cookson ruffled his lad's hair, knowing then that his son's story about finding some tubes sticking out of the ground had only been his over-active imagination.

56

It was Friday night and Jack was sitting in the corner with his pint, waiting for Rachel. The guy with his paper was already there, looking very busy as usual with yet another crossword.

Jack thought it'd been an interesting week to say the least, especially after hearing what Steph had told him about Rachel, her friends, and the business with the gun. They obviously weren't bothered about being seen in public, but the sight of a weapon and Rachel's short but violent reaction was now beginning to niggle him. And the memory of following a woman called Briony into Holborn underground station made his skin prickle.

He looked at his watch. 7.15 p.m. No sign of her. Then, just as he thought perhaps she wasn't coming, he heard her voice, but she sounded slightly pissed.

Having collected a bottle of Prosecco and two glasses from the bar she slowly staggered towards him. He was about to pull a chair out for her, but she sat down at a larger table next to his.

"Not joining us then, Jack?" she joked.

Seeing her like that surprised him and thinking about it for a moment, he nodded, then moved. But he didn't like it there though because he had his back to everyone and thinking about Rachel's friends in the Miners' car park gave him the jitters not being able to see who came in. He didn't know who the other glass was for either.

He was just about to ask when in staggered Michelle and plonked herself down.

Next to him!

She looked more pissed than Rachel too and after she'd sat down she slapped Jack's thigh. He didn't know what to say. Wondered why these two were together. Was she another one of Brendan's family? He didn't know so he kept his mouth tightly closed and listened.

Rachel was about to introduce them, but she began to pour their drinks and after glancing at Michelle several times Jack looked on as the Prosecco was poured into the two glasses. Something was going on. Then Rachel spilt her drink on the floor, so she staggered to the bar and bought another bottle. When she returned, she filled their glasses and the two women lifted them high, making a toast.

"To freedom!" Michelle shrieked in a broad Glaswegian accent.

It was obvious to Jack that he would have to be careful and not ask too many questions, so looking at Rachel he asked what they were celebrating.

Wide-eyed and giggling like women do when they've had a drink or two, Rachel shouted, "She's just got divorced!"

And more cheers were then followed by the obligatory selfies to mark the event's celebration.

In party mood the two women hutched up close together like bosom pals whilst Michelle fished around in her bag for her mobile phone. She messed about with it, looking as though she hadn't a clue what to do with it and watching the phone wobble about at arm's length in front of them Rachel waited for her to say smile. At least three photos were taken which made them both laugh, especially after Michelle showed Rachel the results.

Jack looked on, wondering what the hell Michelle was up to. And sitting out of their way until the selfie-shoot was over, Jack watched Michelle suddenly stand up and move away from the table to take an incoming call. She winked at him as she took the call, but it only lasted a few seconds. She sat down again, muttering something about it being a wrong number and swore.

Then the two women chatted about how the newfound freedom felt and the conversation turned to women-talk which left Jack feeling like the proverbial spare.

He joined in the conversation, but only when he got the chance, and that was proving difficult. These two could talk for England. And probably the rest of the world as well if they chose to. But he was finding it hard not letting on that he knew Michelle.

He turned and looked round the room. He noticed the guy with his crossword staring at them, chewing the inside of his cheek again, only this time he was smirking about something, probably 26 down.

And while the two women chatted, yelled, and drank, Jack picked up one of the beer mats that was on the table and slowly began to tear it up into tiny, tiny pieces. Just something to do. Appeared not to be listening to what the women were jabbering on about.

At times like this he kept his eyes and ears open, but he wasn't looking. Now he was watching. Wasn't just hearing either. He was now listening. Intently. And although the difference is as fine as the thickness of a money-spider's silken thread, it is a very important difference.

Michelle, however, was now staring at Jack's t-shirt that he had on under his open fleece. Didn't seem happy about it.

On it was a circular royal-looking crest with the Queen's crown at its top and in the centre of the circle were a few words:

'We at GCHQ *always* listen to our customers'.

And whilst Rachel was talking, Michelle kept frowning every so often, looking more than once at Jack's T-shirt. And at the man with the crossword.

Ten minutes later and they went back to chatting about the divorce. How long had it taken to come through? How much had it cost? Was it a local solicitor? Was it the absolute? The questions were endless.

Jack, however, sat there tearing up the other beer mats and eventually, when he'd torn six of them up, having pushed the bits into a pile at the centre of the table, he sat back looking towards the restaurant area, listening to the two women whilst glancing at the guy with his crossword.

It was Rachel who first noticed the small pile of beer-soaked cardboard debris on the table.

"Jack! What y'doing?" she slurred.

"Oh sorry Raich," he said, shrugging his shoulders, grinning as he started to move the bits around the table as if they were dominoes.

"Habit," he muttered. "It's just something to do whenever I listen in on other people's conversations."

Rachel shook her head, almost laughing, but for a split second, Michelle looked totally horrified. She closed her mouth quickly and let her face take on its normal appearance. But Jack clocked her reaction and before he could ask her why, she suddenly spun round to face him.

He could almost feel the pain as her eyes drilled holes in his head. She stared at him, screwing her eyes up angrily as she faced him. And looking suspiciously at Jack she quietly growled at him in her broad Glaswegian accent.

"Yooz under fuckn' cover or summat?"

57

"Where y'been, Michael?"

Declan was standing with the old Land Rover's door wide open for Michael to clamber out.

"Just been up on the top to check the ground where the flues were. Looks as though it was like that before the flues were put in. Saw some kids playing up there the other day, so I had to go and remove them. Didn't need them anyway, but I don't want the kids getting too bloody nosey eh?"

Declan helped him unload some large boxes from the back of the vehicle and take them inside.

"Got them from Rachel's lazy bloody partner. You can take a box home with you when you finish work."

"So how's the ditch look now then?"

Michael winked.

"Looks just like there was nothing there."

Declan smiled.

"Should be seeing Sean soon about the gear someone's bringing over. Then we can start to process some of the nasty things that go bang eh?"

Declan followed Michael into one of the smaller offices inside the mill.

58

In the shower, Helen was getting rid of all the smells from the previous night. She let her short flowery dressing gown slip to the floor and looked at her naked body in the full-length mirror that was on the back of the bathroom door. She giggled at her reflection, relieved to see there were no signs of bruising or missing teeth. *Another boring night*, she thought and stepped under the shower.

She hadn't expected Jack to be in the pub with Rachel and she was relieved that he hadn't told Rachel they'd already met, but she wondered how she'd cope on their next run together. She looked forward to it though. Jack was now becoming a bit of an enigma. Might learn more about him if she asked the right questions. And she knew she was very good at that.

Her thoughts then moved to what she'd said to Jack when she'd asked if he were under-cover. She frowned, wondering whether or not he really was. If he wasn't, she'd simply forget all about it. But what disturbed her was that he'd acted so well. Too well.

She thought about it for a few seconds and then shook her head. *Couldn't be*, she told herself, *we'd have been told, wouldn't we?* She thought about it for a few seconds more as she poured some shampoo from the bottle onto her hair.

Wouldn't we?

It began to worry her and, suddenly, a different thought rushed into her head. And that *really* worried her.

Could he be on the other side?

After about ten minutes she drew back the shower curtain and stepped out. She looked at herself again in the mirror and ran her fingers through her wet short hair, admiring herself. *Still looking good though babe*, she smiled. And a little later, after getting dried, she wandered into her bedroom to find something to wear.

From the drawer in the bottom of her wardrobe she found her old jeans and a pretty top. Couldn't find the thong she wanted so she had to make do with a pair of panties instead. Not her best ones though. Wouldn't dream of wearing *them* with jeans. *They* were for special occasions. To be worn only under a dress or a skirt. She slipped the old ones on and stood barefoot in the bedroom. Then she looked at the clock on the bedside table.

"Bollocks!" she shouted. "C'mon girl. Get a move on!"

Whilst making sure she looked OK to go out she looked for some socks but could only find odd ones. One said Monday, the other had Thursday on it.

"They'll do. No one's going to notice," she said as she put them on.

And last of all she pulled on her old pair of trainers.

Grabbing the bag she'd had the night before, and the coat she'd worn before, she locked the door and ran down the stairs. Once she was outside, she looked at her watch.

"Twenty minutes," she whistled.

59

After walking across the mini roundabout near Morrisons on Saturday morning, someone in a car pipped their horn, making Jack turn to see who it was, but he was too late and all he saw was the back end of it disappearing up the road. He was just going round the corner and heading into Brook Street when someone tapped him on his shoulder. He turned around to face a very dishevelled-looking Rachel. Through bleary eyes she looked at him and gave him a silly grin.

"Coffee somewhere?" she asked wearily. It wasn't really a question, sounded more like a plea.

Jack pecked her on the cheek, took her arm, and slowly guided her up the street to Nero's. Still wasn't sure if she'd been the woman he, Fiona, and Greg had followed.

Inside they sat at the back where Jack ordered a latte for her and a hot chocolate for himself. He looked at her.

"Y'been home yet?"

He couldn't help asking. After all, she looked bloody rough.

"Yes I have if you must know," she scowled. "I was coming to pick my car up. Left it outside your place after work yesterday."

"Hadn't noticed," he lied.

"Yeah, well I'd been for a drink in Cellars Bar with some friends after work, then, just before they left, that Glaswegian cow joined us."

Jack kept a straight face. *Cow eh?* he smiled to himself, *better not let **her** hear you say that.* Rachel sighed then continued, "And that was when we saw you in The Bridge. Reckon we'd had a bit too much to drink by then though."

She chuckled naughtily.

Jack nodded, knowing what she meant. And putting some sugar in her latte, she stirred it round and round.

"Still feel like a bag of shit," she moaned.

Jack laughed at her.

"Well," he told her, "you're the loveliest bag of shit I've ever seen."

She smiled at the complement and lifted the cup to her lips.

"So who was she then?" Jack asked.

"Haven't a bloody clue. Just joined up with us in Cellars Bar, why, d'y'fancy her?"

"Well she could bring my tea to me in bed."

Rachel laughed at his rude remark and looked at her watch.

"Jesus Christ!" she exclaimed. "Supposed to be meeting her in the pub for some lunch."

"Where, The Bridge?"

She nodded and finished her coffee.

"Join you?" Jack asked before draining the hot chocolate down his throat.

"Mmmm, why not," she replied and kissed him slowly.

On both cheeks.

60

They made it to the pub between the showers of rain, having rushed as best they could, knowing how bad Rachel was feeling, and once inside they looked around. Didn't see anyone they knew.

Buying their drinks, they went to sit down in the corner, but Rachel got there first and sat in Jack's seat. Again. Once more it put him on edge, and he didn't like it.

"When're you supposed to be meeting her?"

"Now," she moaned, looking at the clock above the bar.

"Sure you got the right pub?" he said, taking the piss.

But she was in no mood for his jokes.

"Ow!"

Rachel's fist had just said hello to his right shoulder, and it had hurt him too, so he rubbed it hard before taking a sip of his pint. Once again, she had unknowingly found his weak spot and together with her punch and the rainy weather, his shoulders were giving him jip again.

Jack had tried not to let her see how much it had hurt him and she didn't know it had.

"So, what's your friend's name then, Rachel?" he asked.

Jack saw her smiling.

She looked at him and nodded towards the bar.

"Why don't you ask her yourself?"

"Eh?"

"She's just this minute come in."

61

The Major's voice was clear and assertive.

"There's an old mill near there Cass. Millmeece I think it was called. Derelict now though. Took water from the River Meece via a narrow run they had to make when they built the mill a long time ago. Empties back out into the river further downstream. The mill fell into disrepair after the owners died. Sorry to say, there are no plans of the place, so we've simply drawn a blank."

He paused and cleared his throat. Cassie stood next to him looking at the large map that was spread out across the top of the large table. He pointed to the place on the map they were talking about.

"Even the OS maps show nothing there. Reckon the locals thereabouts should know more about it, so try the nearby pubs or one of those quaint tea-rooms you find nestled peacefully up there."

Cassie sighed.

"D'you reckon it's the likely place though, Gov?"

The Major coughed a couple of times.

"Not too sure at the moment, Cass, but ask around first and if nothing comes up, go and have a look at it. Like I said, it's derelict now, but if there is a noise coming from it, someone's using it. Let me know what you find though. And don't rush. There's no hurry. Yet."

They said cheerio to each other and when Cassie left the office, she dialled her friend.

62

"Reckon I'm going to have to get my field-craft up to scratch soon."

"Why?" Helen asked.

Pete chuckled.

"Your friendly runner might be in trouble."

"How d'you mean?"

"Got a bit of info on him from those photos you took."

"Good or bad?"

"Shall I say it's certainly *not* what we'd've expected."

"Sound interesting," she mused.

"Mmmm. It is."

"You'll have to let me know when I get in then. Could give you a hand with the field-craft as well if you like?"

Pete laughed at the thought.

"Oh thanks. But no thanks. I'll be OK," he told her.

"But how did you get his photo without him seeing?"

Helen sniggered.

"Oh c'mon. I pretended to take a call and moved away from the table. Whilst I chatted to no one I took his photo on my mobile."

"You sneaky mare."

"How are you going to help him then?"

"Probably catch him in the pub. Let you know later."

Pete put the phone down and sat back in his chair, smirking to himself.

63

Back in the pub Jack had been too interested in Rachel and hadn't seen her friend come in. Couldn't. He was facing the wrong way.

Putting his pint down Jack turned around as Rachel's friend from Friday walked straight over to them and sat down next to him, but turning round to look at her had made his shoulder ache again. He began to rub it.

"Hi," the woman beamed and gave Jack's knee another hard slap as she sat down. He looked down at her hand.

"He wants to know your name," Rachel joked.

Embarrassed wasn't the word.

"Oh, did I not say?" she asked as innocently as she could. "I'm Michelle."

Jack shook hands and said hello, giving her a tiny wink.

Rachel introduced him, but Michelle just laughed. Called him Duvet. Rachel laughed as well, but Jack's face had a question mark right across it.

"What?" he demanded.

"Duvet," Michelle said again. "Joke. Y'know, under-cover?"

He got it OK and he also got that she must have given it some thought. He'd told her he wasn't, and he could see she still didn't look too sure. And from the face she was pulling, neither did Rachel.

The conversation changed to what they were going to have for lunch, but the look on Rachel's face said she wouldn't be having very much, if anything at all. He handed a menu to them though and Michelle proceeded to look through it, almost salivating at the thought of what there was to eat.

She was just about to stand up and go to the bar, but Jack beat her to it.

"More drinks?" he asked.

Silly question.

And when they nodded, he walked over to the bar to order the meals and drinks, but just as he was about to carry the drinks back to their table, Jack suddenly found himself standing face to face with the guy who did the crossword. He'd just returned his empty glass and was blocking his way. Whilst trying to think where he'd appeared from, they both moved the same way to avoid each other, like they were dancing. They laughed and the guy muttered sorry, but as he turned, he brushed against Jack and walked quickly out of the pub.

Jack was now thinking fast. *That* was the third time he'd bumped into him that week and when Jack got back with the drinks he told his friends what had just happened. Told them he'd done it before as well, which made them both laugh, but Michelle's eyes were threatening him and held his for a moment.

It was an unusually long moment and it got Jack wondering if she too was part of what had just occurred. He twisted round in his seat, frowning at her. Asking. Questioning the look she'd given him.

She noticed.

And quick as a flash she nudged his arm.

"Better check your pockets then, Jack. Y'know, under-cover. Just like they do in those spy films. Remember?"

A crafty smile whipped across her face as she winked at him.

Jack understood her message straight away and moved his head up and down so slowly, so discreetly, no one else but Michelle caught it.

At the same time, totally unaware of what had taken place, Rachel laughed at what Michelle had said. Thought it was very funny.

It hadn't taken Jack very long to cotton on to what had happened, so he decided to go for a pee.

Inside the cubicle, he felt in his pockets and found a piece of paper in one of them. He took it out and read it.

'Rachel's dangerous. She's your enemy, Jack!'

He stood there speechless, trying to fathom out why the guy was warning him about her. He knew she might have had a gun, but these days, even though it was illegal, lots of people carried them.

But what did the guy know about Rachel though? What the hell did he know about *him*? Who the fuck was he? But he knew who Michelle was. Or he thought he did.

Returning to his table as he walked through the restaurant area, Jack wondered if he was with his people.

He had an idea, but he wasn't going to ask next time he saw him in the pub. Jack was going to have lunch with two women and he wasn't going to let anything spoil that, even if one of them was supposed to be dangerous. He smiled to himself, wondering if *that* could refer to both of them.

An hour later, when they'd finished their lunches, Michelle leaned back in her chair, patted her stomach or what there was of it, and puffed her cheeks out.

"Stuffed," she sighed.

Jack laughed, but Rachel wasn't looking too good. She was looking pale and had hardly eaten anything.

"Anyone want another drink?" he asked casually, but the two women simply shook their heads.

"Would love to, Jack," Rachel began, "but I still don't feel well. Besides I've got to drop some work off for a friend."

Michelle frowned as Rachel got up.

"You'll be OK on your own?" Jack asked, pretending to be

concerned about her health, whilst wondering if the work she was dropping off was in the shape of another firearm.

"Don't worry, Jack. I'll walk down the road back to my car, thanks. The fresh air will probably make me feel better."

She picked her things up, said cheerio, and left the pub.

Now that they were alone Jack gave Michelle a serious look.

"What the fuck are you and the guy with the paper up to, eh?"

Blinking innocently, she shook her head.

"Don't know what you mean, Jack. I just wanted her to go so I could have you *all* to myself."

And she tickled him playfully as if she fancied him.

"You can't fool me, Michelle," Jack suddenly said.

She looked amazed.

"Don't know what you mean."

"Don't come the innocent, Michelle. Your accent's good, but you seemed to know more than you're letting on when your friend barged into me," he said angrily. "You both work together, don't you?"

She didn't speak for a few seconds, then she looked down at the table, embarrassed.

"Shit!"

It sounded like an admission and without another word being spoken they left the pub.

Walking along the canal path Jack suddenly grabbed her arm.

"What happened back there wasn't just a coincidence, was it?"

She frowned, wondering what he knew.

"Not sure where you're going, Jack," she said slowly.

But her eyes were smiling at him.

"You're both with the security services, aren't you? You're a bloody spook, Michelle, or whatever your name is."

In a moment of anger, she grabbed Jack's hand as though she was about to break his wrist, but she stopped in time. He thought she was going to kiss him. But she didn't. And even though she very much wanted to, she also very much wanted to smash him in the face and drop him in the canal.

Jack was waiting to hear what she was going to say. Waiting to see if she'd finally admit it.

"Why d'you think I work for them?" she asked angrily.

"Did it m'self, that's why!"

Jack's comment stopped her dead in her tracks, but her poker face didn't change, and they walked back to Jack's place very quickly. Very silently.

"Coming in for a drink to discuss it then?"

She looked in shock.

"Sorry, Jack. Not now!"

64

On Monday morning, after finding another circular stuck, this time under one of his car's windscreen wipers, Jack put it in his pocket and went to work.

Once he was home though, he took the circular out of his pocket and studied it. Another set of letters and numbers were written on it and he knew it was another code:

S19/11-16/4-07/3:91.

Jack scratched his head trying to remember what they could be and whilst pouring himself a glass of whisky the numbers slowly began to reveal their meaning. ˙

He went into the lounge and pulled an ordnance survey map off one of the shelves of the bookcase, unfolded it, and pored over it.

The time of the meeting was the last two numbers and the colon meant they were to be read back to front. 91 became19. The other parts fell into place straight away. They were grid references.

Specific ones.

65

"Weren't you supposed to be spending a few nights in Nottingham then?"

Rachel's eyebrows almost joined together as Declan put some cups and saucers near the kitchen sink, waiting for her to reply.

Shaking her head she told him that when she'd seen her partner earlier, she'd had to revise her story, pretending that her trip had been postponed, telling him instead that she had to meet her boss later. And he'd just accepted it.

Declan laughed.

"Don't know how you get away with it."

She laughed.

"I lie a lot," she smirked. "'S'what I do."

"Looks like you've spent the night on the bloody tiles though, kid."

"Mmmm don't remind me, Dec."

She sniffed.

"Got a good look at him though, but I don't think it's the guy I want. He's certainly not dangerous. Reckon Pat and Con just don't know how to bloody fight."

She opened a bottle of wine.

"You sure?" he asked. "He might have sussed you out."

Rachel pulled a face, thinking about it.

"Sussed me out? Don't think so, Dec," she said. "But there were a couple of things I didn't like."

She then began to tell him about the t-shirt and he took it all on board.

"He's nothing like the guy I pretended to shoot that night and he hasn't got that scar we were told about either."

"Not to worry, girl. The guy you're looking for *was* in that scrap."

"Not this one, Dec," she laughed. "He couldn't fight his way out of a paper-fuckin'-bag let alone get into a scrap and win, believe me. Reckon Pat and Con need lessons."

She poured the wine out and sampled it.

"And he'll definitely have some sort of scar," Declan went on. "But it's probably faded by now anyway."

Rachel sipped her wine.

"Mmm this is quite nice, love. Where did it come from?"

Declan put an arm round her waist and kissed her. She waited for him to answer her question, even though she knew exactly what he was going to say.

He sipped his wine and raised his glass to meet hers.

"Chateau de Paul."

66

It was almost midnight by the time Greg had parked the car near the river, about a mile from the mill. He and Cassie waited a few moments for their eyes to adjust to the darkness before setting off along the riverbank, keeping well away from the gravel road that led to the derelict mill.

They heard the noise of the millstream long before they saw it. Sounded like they were near some rapids, but when they reached them, they realised, even in the dark, that the water was quite shallow, and the noise was caused by the volume of water rushing over some large stones in the middle.

They walked on until they came to a length of rusting 6ft wire-netting fence stretched between several concrete posts. They stopped and looked at the dangling sign that was almost in two halves, hanging diagonally from a nail bent round the wire.

'Danger! Keep Out!' ordered the faded red words in the dim light from Cassie's torch, but neither she nor Greg heard its command and, standing for a few seconds, looking at the sign, they smiled at each other and agreed.

Disobeying the sign's command, they went through the gap in the fence. It was large enough to drive a bus through and Greg shook his head. If this place was being used by terrorists to make bombs it seemed a well-chosen spot and it also wasn't where anyone would suspect anything.

They made their way towards the mill and further on, they found the road leading to the mill's entrance. Where it had left the main road it was just a gravel track, but now, this road had a new surface.

Cassie and Greg stopped for a few seconds and listened. Apart from the sound of rushing water, everything around them was quiet.

They followed the road round a bend where they were given their first view of the derelict mill standing before them some hundred yards away. Its stone edifice, half-in, half-out of the hill-side, was barely visible, but an old street light nearby that looked like it was on its last legs, added a yellow tinge to the stone, illuminating the mill as though it might have been an old ruined house belonging to the National Trust. And another light could be seen too.

The mill was in use.

67

It was raining hard by the time Jack drove off to meet Greg. At the traffic lights at the top of the hill a couple of hundred yards up the road he turned left and headed off towards the village of Armitage, a couple of miles or so away.

He drove steadily passed the meeting place and into the village. He didn't see anything out of the ordinary and, having doubled back, he parked his car opposite the pub on the spare ground in front of a large mobile-residential site.

He watched and waited.

Then, several minutes later, Greg parked his car at the pub and looked across the road towards Jack's car. Its windscreen wipers were halfway across the windscreen.

Everything was safe.

Seeing Jack, Greg touched his nose before going into the pub whereupon Jack crossed the road and met his friend at 7 p.m. as planned.

There weren't many cars outside The Plumbers even though it was Wednesday, but once inside they realised how full the place was and turning right they went to sit in a corner of the almost empty restaurant area before ordering their drinks.

When the waitress brought them both a menu they ordered cokes, then she left them for a few minutes to choose something to eat.

Sitting side by side, neither Jack nor Greg said a word until the meals were placed in front of them and the waitress had returned to the bar. From their table they both had a good view of anyone coming into the pub through the front door. But they couldn't from the entrance at the back though. That was a risk they'd have to take. After all, no one would have known they were going to be there.

Throughout the meal they caught up on what they were both doing, but Jack couldn't believe he was being asked if he'd like to return to the Firm and work there again.

Greg worried him when he told Jack that two others were now watching him closely. Didn't want to say who they were either. Not just then. But Jack had a good idea and related the story that Steph had told him about the gun incident with Rachel and friends.

"Don't think you realise, Jack, but she's the woman we followed into Holborn station."

Greg's words made Jack gasp. Although *that* had crossed his mind, he found it difficult to understand how she was so close to him again.

Greg then went on to explain how she'd been picked up by GCHQ again, but this time in Bristol, after which they found out that she was related to the guy he put in prison.

"Oh my God!"

Jack hung his head in his hands and sighed deeply. Couldn't believe it. Greg saw his friend's reaction.

"Gets worse though, mate."

Jack looked up, wondering what was coming next.

"I've been over to Dublin a few times and although we've no idea what she and her friends are planning, all we do know is that it's something big. And we may have found their bomb-making factory too."

They continued to eat their meals whilst Greg informed Jack about what they'd found.

"So are you up for it, Jack?"

"I'll have to have time to think about it all first, Greg."

"Don't worry, I'll let the Major know, but don't be surprised if he only offers you a desk job. I mean we can't let you go running about with your leg like it is eh?"

What his friend had just said hurt more than his leg did, but he knew he was right.

"I appreciate that, Greg. Just keep in contact though eh?"

Greg nodded and from his pocket he took out a mobile phone.

"It's yours, Jack. And it's encrypted so you'll be safe to call me, OK?"

Jack looked at the phone and slipped it into his coat pocket.

"Thanks Greg."

Eventually, after they'd finished their meals and Jack had paid the bill, they shook hands before leaving the pub one at a time, three minutes apart. And looking through one of the pub's windows Jack watched as Greg got into his car to head off into the village of Armitage. But just as Greg was about to leave the car park, a car coming along the road from Rugeley slowed down and for no reason let him out. It then followed Greg's car.

And Jack realised that it was the same one that had pipped at him few days ago.

68

Cassie and Greg slowly edged their way towards the mill, keeping silently and carefully in step with each other. Should anyone have heard them, the sound would have been of only one person, not two.

Eventually, they saw the mill's huge archway where the stream poured out of it. Inside its entrance, the old wooden millwheel was still slowly and relentlessly grumbling, forced to turn by the pressure of the fast-flowing water.

The archway looked like the top half of a large open mouth and to its right was a single door within a much larger one. Similar in design to an aircraft hangar's door, but this one was made of wood, not metal.

A light could be seen coming from the gap in the smaller door, so Cassie and Greg approached it with caution only to find another entrance, some twenty yards away, almost hidden out of sight by the curve of the rounded hillside.

This other entrance had a large door that was made of thick metal and had been made to slide open sideways across the newly built road. Once again there was a smaller door within the large one and it was slightly open.

When they reached it, Cassie looked first at its hinges. They were well oiled, so she gave the door a gentle push. Not a sound was produced. She peered through the widened gap, tugging Greg's sleeve, allowing him to take a look too.

Having squeezed through the gap in the doorway they found themselves in a sort of cavern that was next to the mill. They could see the very large and partly broken millwheel that was still moaning to itself as it slowly rotated, and attached to a series of gear-wheels were broad worn leather straps that disappeared into the darkness above. And going through a nearby wall to drive something else further inside, were other straps.

But these were newly made ones.

69

"He said what?"

Pete's voice rose higher and higher.

"Reckoned I was a spook," Helen shot back. "Wasn't pissing about either, Pete. Not sure if he isn't one himself."

"Why would he have said that?"

"Said he'd been one once."

Pete coughed then cleared his voice.

"Mmmm. He was though, Helen. Still might be too. Don't know yet."

He paused, turned in his chair, and took a file from the top of the small office-cabinet.

"Got this yesterday from a friend."

He pushed the file across the desktop. Helen looked suspicious but interested. Didn't know what to say. She opened the file and began to read it.

"Christ Pete! And we've been thinking he was tied up with that bloody woman."

Pete suddenly guffawed loudly.

"He'd have probably liked that," he joked.

Helen shook her head.

"Trust you to think that."

"Just goes to show how much we don't know though, doesn't it?"

"Well I've got to say when I asked him that night about being under-cover, he didn't seem to let it worry him."

"Wouldn't have though, would he? He's good. He's a pro, Helen.

One of the best I was told. Worried you, didn't it?"

Helen stopped reading and closed the file quickly.

"I suppose so, but he did such a good job of it. Anyway, at least my gut feelings were right, weren't they?"

Pete chuckled and put the file away in one of the cabinet drawers.

"So what're we going to do now?"

70

Wanting to get to know more about him during a run one morning, Michelle had asked Jack to go back to her flat. He also wanted to know what she was up to and accepted her invitation. After work. 7 p.m.

"And don't be late," she joked, tapping her watch again.

Her flat was on the edge of town, in a two-storey block of four flats. Michelle's was one of the upstairs ones and below her, she told him, lived an elderly couple. The other three flats were also occupied by elderly people as well, which made him wonder how come she was in one. But he didn't dare ask her.

They went up the stairs, through the 'front' door as she called it and into a short hallway from which the other rooms branched off. There were two bedrooms, a decent sized lounge, a kitchen, and a bathroom. Jack commented on how nice a place it was and, even though it was dark outside, he told her how he thought the view from the kitchen window must have been pleasant because it looked over a small park with bushes and trees nearby. The flat looked very expensive too, but he didn't ask.

She showed him round, but to Jack it didn't look lived in. Well, not as much as he'd imagined it should have. There were no pictures on the walls. No photos of friends or family anywhere to be seen. Not a thing. There were none of the usual things that women put in bedrooms or bathrooms. There was nothing in the lounge either. No magazines or papers. Not a thing.

Even the windowsills were clutter free. He liked that though. In fact, the entire place looked more like a show-home. It lacked the character of someone actually living there. She evidently noticed and told him again that she'd recently moved up from Bristol.

"Oh. Whereabouts?" he asked her.

"Near Yate."

But Jack wasn't convinced.

He followed her into the kitchen, and they waited for the kettle to boil so they could have some coffee.

"So why are *you* watching Rachel?"

"Thought you'd've known that, Jack."

"I do. That's how my leg got injured."

The kettle boiled and Michelle made the coffee.

"So where d'you work then?" she asked, changing the subject.

"Roger's Transport," he said. "I'm the accounts manager."

"Mmmmm. Accounts manager eh? And what does your firm haul then?" she asked purely out of curiosity. And the need to know.

Jack told her and added that they handled just about anything they could. It was that sort of business. Get what you can, when you can.

"Anything you're not supposed to?" she asked.

Jack laughed.

"Nothing secret, if that's what you mean," he replied.

And after they'd gone into the lounge, Jack asked Michelle about her work.

"So what's the woman up to now then, Michelle?" he demanded.

"Thought your friend might have told you the other night in The Plumbers."

"How d'you know about that?"

Michelle thought about it for a moment.

"Well, since you're evidently still with six, I can tell you, but it's still our op, Jack."

"What d'you mean still with six?"

"Oh Jack, I'd have thought you of all people would have known. You never leave the security services."

"Still doesn't explain what's happening though. I haven't a bloody clue."

"Just stay like you are when you're in the pub with her, Jack. But don't start to get too friendly. Word has it that she wants to kill you for getting Brendan O'Shea banged up."

They sipped their coffee.

"And what's with the guy who does his crossword in the pub then?"

"Oh y'mean Pete? He watches and listens when he can. He's also got friends elsewhere."

"Ahhh. Now things are becoming clearer. I thought he was guarding Rachel to start with."

Michelle laughed.

"No Jack. He's the one who's told me about you. Only a bit. Expect he's finding out more as we speak."

She took their empty cups and put them on the draining board.

"And that's about as much as I can say at the moment, Jack. So please, not a word to anyone, OK?"

As he stood up to go home Michelle gave him a kiss on his cheek.

"Are you wearing make-up, Jack?"

71

Coming towards a small office-like building within the mill's cavernous space near to where Cassie and Greg were hiding, a middle-aged guy in a chemist's long but dirty white coat had just appeared from another of the breeze block offices that were dotted around inside this illuminated cave.

On his head was a raised up protective face-shield and in one gloved hand he was holding a sheet of paper, looking at it as though something on it wasn't quite right. In the other hand though was a six-inch tall glass flask which appeared to have liquid in it. From the flask they could see what looked like steam coming out of it and it was evaporating almost immediately. Greg knew that something in the flask was either very hot or very cold, but not poisonous.

He almost gasped, horrified at what the man might be making, but Cassie tapped his shoulder, shaking her head and giving him her famous look.

Shut the fuck up!

They relaxed a little as the man shuffled out of the office and into one of the others. When the door had been closed, Cassie crept under the window and peered through it.

In front of her was what looked like a small laboratory.

72

Jack had had a phone call in the office, but he was already taking a call, so his credit controller Anne had taken it instead. When he'd ended his call, she passed hers through to him and whilst it was ringing, he looked across at her and mouthed 'who is it?' She pulled a face and shrugged her shoulders. Jack picked his phone up.

"Good morning," he said, going into his usual line, "Roger's Transport, Jack Mason speaking."

A woman giggled.

"Good morning Mr Mason," the very posh voice said.

"Er, who's speaking please?" he asked politely.

"Oh c'mon now, Jack, you can't have forgotten already, can you?"

She sounded different that day. He teased her, but then he wondered how she knew his work's number. Then he realised *they* knew everything. Well almost. He knew he hadn't given it to her.

"Hello Michelle or whatever you're called," he said, joking about the uncertainty of not knowing her real name.

"You alone?"

Jack put the phone down on his desk, got up, and closed the door.

"Am now, why?"

"I have to talk to you."

73

"Came through about half an hour ago," Pete said as he threw the folder across the table for Helen to read.

She picked it up, looked at him, and opened the file. A broad crafty grin was spreading across his face.

She'd only read a couple of paragraphs on the first page of the new file when she suddenly stopped and looked at him.

"Oh my God!" she exclaimed. "Never realised he'd been with *that* lot."

Pete's head moved up and down slowly whilst Helen read on.

"Yeah," he smirked. "Funny thing is though, quite a few authors turned him into a fictional character when they wrote spy stories about the Balkan conflict. Didn't mention him by name, of course, but made him a secret agent based loosely on what Jack had been doing during that particular war."

Helen sipped her coffee as she continued to read the file.

"He did quite a lot of work like that too."

"How d'you mean?"

"Don't you know?"

Helen shrugged her shoulders.

"Before my time," she joked.

"Well," he began. "Some members of 'that lot', as you called them, actually penetrated Bosnia's security service. Jack turned one of their top people and brought him over to our side when the conflict ended."

"You're joking."

Pete laughed.

"If you don't believe me read the books yourself, girl. There's plenty of them."

He smiled before continuing.

"Thing is, he got caught up in that London Underground bombing a few years ago. Was almost killed. He's still on the firm's books though. Never resigned. Wasn't discharged. Anyway, I just thought I'd let you know so you don't get into a scrap with him."

He laughed at the thought. Helen's scowl told him to be careful.

"I'll keep an eye on him while you're in town enjoying that romantic view from the boss's office," he continued sarcastically. "He'll probably feel safer now, considering that he knows."

She raised an eyebrow.

"How d'you mean, safer?"

"Greg's a mate of his."

"Eh?"

"Mmmm. Couldn't believe it myself. Evidently go back a long way, young lady. In the Balkans together."

"Bloody hell! And here we were thinking Jack was one of the bad guys."

"That depends which side you're on."

"Still can't believe it," she said. "Well, I'll give him the Scotland story, so he'll not expect to see me around for a while."

Pete nodded his head.

"But in the meantime," she added, "I've an appointment with some people near Hereford. See you later."

74

"Go on then," he said, "you planning something?"

There was a moment's silence. There always is when such a question is asked.

"Not really, Jack," she said. "Got to go away for a week or so, that was all. Just thought it polite to let you know."

"What? A week or so?" he gasped. "Where y'going?"

"Oh only up to Ullapool, in the Highlands. Going to see my old Mum. Fly up to Inverness on Tuesday."

"Don't believe a word you're telling me, 'cos I know you'll be up to something else."

He paused, waiting for some comment or other, but there was none. Jack was thinking on his feet now. It was only four days away.

"I'll come and wave cheerio then," he joked.

"That's very nice of you, Jack, but I'd prefer it if you didn't. I might get all emotional," she said, trying to stop herself from giggling.

"How about we meet in the pub tonight then?"

"OK. I won't be able to get there until about eight though."

And the phone call suddenly ended.

Although Michelle hadn't sounded very sad about going away, Jack was very much looking forward to seeing her again. He was really falling head over heels in love with her, hoping they could do more than just jog together too. But there were still some questions he had to ask her.

So too did she now. Lots of them.

75

They were having a few drinks, chatting about Michelle's forthcoming trip to Scotland.

"Are you staying up there with your Mum then?" Jack asked.

"No. She's in a home so I'll be staying in a hotel."

"Well I'm sure you'll have a great time, kid. Ullapool. All those fishermen."

"Mmmm, and all that bloody fish too," she joked, giving him the eye, but Jack was thinking more about other things fishy.

"Going to miss me then?" she asked, stroking his hand.

"Too bloody right I am," he told her. "I mean, we're getting on fairly well and I enjoy being in your company. In fact I—"

She didn't let him finish.

"You what? Come on, tell me."

Jack held Michelle's hand.

"Just going to say I hope it continues when you get back."

She pecked him on the cheek again.

"Me too," she said excitedly, hoping her visit to the Stirling Lines at Credenhill wouldn't take long.

They sipped their drinks.

"You'll be speaking Scottish if you stay up there too long."

"Speak it already, Jack. Fluently, remember?"

They laughed about the night she'd joined Rachel.

"Got any more secrets you want to tell me?"

"Theagamh," she purred softly in Gaelic. "Perhaps."

Made him wonder what she knew about him then.

"At least I can always call you on your mobile or text you eh?"

And whilst they exchanged their mobile numbers, Michelle leaned across the table. Some of the things she'd recently read about him were now swirling round in her head. That fight in Bristol for instance that he'd not really told her about. So, she began to look closely at his face.

Smiling at him, moving forward in her chair and reaching out to let her fingers gently stroke the right-hand side of his face, she frowned.

"Mmmm. Bit of a scar there, Jack," she whispered. "Hadn't noticed it before."

76

It was quite late on Friday night when Jack turned the key in the lock of his front door. He and Michelle had got drenched in a heavy downpour as they'd walked along the road from the pub and now they were both thoroughly wet through. She still hadn't told him her real name and was hoping he wouldn't ask.

She waited in the hallway while he switched a light on, then, she went straight in, managing not to trip over her case that she was taking to Ullapool. She'd dropped it off after she'd finished work before they went to the pub.

Jack threw her a towel to dry her hair on, hung her wet things with his by the radiator in the kitchen, and then went into the lounge to pour them both a whisky.

Before Jack could pass the glass to her, she flung her arms round his neck and kissed him. Hard. She seemed to be enjoying it, so he let her carry on.

"What's the whisky?" she asked when they'd pulled apart.

"Bunnahabhain. Single malt from the Isle of Islay," he told her.

"Mmmm, nice," she replied, "love that peaty taste."

He was about to draw the curtains in the lounge, but she insisted on leaving them open. He didn't mind. He turned the lights down low and told her if anyone could see them from across the canal on the tow path at that time of night, good luck to them.

They only had the one drink though. Michelle wanted to go to bed. She'd told Jack she was tired. Said she'd been up since 4 a.m. Probably had. Now with a better idea of what she actually did, he knew it meant working anytime of the day or night.

He carried her case upstairs and put it in the spare room whilst she went to the bathroom, but just as he was about to draw the bedroom curtains, he heard her voice.

"Jack, there's no bloody light in here."

He found a small torch that he kept on the bedside table for such occasions and handed it to her. Then she wanted something from her case. Jack waited until she'd got whatever it was she looking for, telling her to leave the bathroom door open and he'd leave the landing light on. That way she wouldn't need the torch, and after some huffing and puffing, she emerged in her PJs. He thought she looked irresistible in them, but he didn't get chance to investigate because she rushed past him and jumped into bed as he was switching the landing lights off.

In the dark Jack tried to climb into bed.

"Wrong side, Michelle," he muttered, waiting for her to move across the bed.

"Not now it isn't," she sniggered as she pulled the duvet up to her nose. "Lady's privilege."

And she stayed there, gripping the duvet even tighter, making Jack get in on the other side.

He hated having to sleep that side. Having been kicked in the face too many times had made his left nostril close up when he slept on his right side. Meant that he had to breathe through his mouth. Turning over so he could breathe better, he placed one hand on her shoulder. Her hand found his, but only for a few minutes, then she simply said good night and let go of it.

He tried to sleep but couldn't. It was impossible. This gorgeous woman was in bed next to him.

Arousing him.

77

Throughout the weekend Michelle kept asking him how he'd got the scar on his face, so eventually, he told her about the fight he'd been in, but he didn't tell her how or why it had started. She wondered then, why he hadn't wanted to tell her. She'd read only a bit about the fight. No doubt if she really wanted to find out Pete would tell her.

She still didn't really know the ins and outs of what she'd read about him in that last file either, but during the night her fingers had discovered the large patches of hard, thick, twisted skin across Jack's back.

Thoughts of how much pain he must have been in when he was in hospital brought tears to her eyes. Made her want to throw up too. She swallowed hard. And although she knew how he'd got the scars, she certainly never realised just how bad they were. She wasn't going to ask either.

Some things were best left unsaid.

78

When Rachel got back home to her partner's house later that evening, she hung her coat up. She heard him running a bath upstairs.

"Hi love," she shouted up to him. "Want me to come up and scrub your back?"

She didn't hear his reply because the house phone started ringing.

"Rachel Stansfield," she said.

"Oh hi, Raich, is Paul in?"

When she heard Jack's voice her heartbeat began to race for a second or two.

"Sorry Jack, he's in the bath, shall I get him to call you back?"

There was a pause.

"Er, no. I'll call him tomorrow, Raich. It's not important."

"So what're *you* doing then?" she whispered mischievously.

"Nothing much, why?"

"Well," she began, keeping her voice quiet. "Since that bloody transport manager of yours doesn't want his back washing, I er was wondering perhaps I could come around and wash yours instead."

There was a long pause.

"If you wanted me to that is," she added sexily.

There was another pause.

"Remind me to let you know next time I'm having a bath then, Raich."

He heard her giggling before the line went dead, leaving them both wondering if either of them would.

"Who was it?" Paul shouted down from the bathroom.

"Oh, only Jack. Said he'd give you a call tomorrow. Wasn't important."

And waiting for the splashing to begin again, Rachel looked at the number that was on the phone. Jack's mobile number. She couldn't resist the opportunity and quickly taking out her mobile she added Jack's number to her phone.

Under the name of Alison she put Jack's number into her list of contacts. Paul would never see it. If he did though, Alison would just be another one of her female friends he'd never met.

79

By Tuesday Jack was all over the place. Michelle was flying off to Inverness. Paul had been moaning that Rachel was always away. Seemed to be enjoying it though, especially since they weren't getting on with each other. And Jack was left thinking about what he'd do on his own.

Whilst Michelle was taking a shower, she'd left her bags and clothes she was taking to Ullapool strewn across the bed, leaving his bedroom looking like that of a thirteen-year-old.

Jack smiled to himself, looking at all the clothes she was taking with her. There were enough to last a year or more. She evidently didn't pack lightly. *But then*, he asked himself, *what woman does?* He wondered if the airline would let her carry so much.

Just as he was about to move her things downstairs, Jack looked at the small cabin-bag that was in between her suitcase and her open handbag. He noticed her passport lying on the bed next to it.

Being nosey, he picked it up, flicked through the pages to see if she'd travelled anywhere interesting, then, turning to the page with her photo on it, hoping it was as funny as everyone else's, he stared at it in disbelief.

80

Just as Steph wandered back to her desk, Jack's boss came in, looked across at him, and jerked his head in the direction of his office.

"Got a minute please, Jack?"

Once they were in the office Mr Adams looked at Jack.

"Well Jack, what's your opinion?"

He shook his head and sighed. The documents he'd been given the week before had suggested that extra fuel was being used unnecessarily and Mr Adams didn't like it.

"The mileages don't relate to some of the journeys the drivers are doing, Roger. Looks like someone's doing other trips."

Roger closed the file that Jack had been looking at all week and nodded his head.

"Glad we agree, Jack," he said, leaning back in his chair, making his fingers into church spires on his chest. "So what d'you think we should do about it?"

His head tilted to one side. Answers please, it was asking.

"Reckon we'll have to monitor it," Jack suggested. "See if there's a pattern, you know, which jobs, which vehicles, which drivers. There's got to be a third party involved too. There usually is."

Mr Adams smiled and leaned forward, resting his elbows on the top of his desk, hands still together as if in prayer while he listened to Jack's theories.

"Glad to know we're reading from the same page, Jack."

And picking the file up off his desk he turned and put it on a pile of others that were on a table next to him. He closed his eyes and nodded at Jack.

His signal to leave.

And as Jack walked out of the office, the boss's secretary Mandy was about to go in. As they passed each other by the door Jack heard the boss say, 'thanks Jack'.

All the way to his office Jack couldn't help wonder what Paul had been doing to miss the excessive mileages like that. Wondered why his own figures and graphs hadn't flagged up anything either because the extra miles had meant picking up extra fuel.

He began looking at the figures on his computer. Still looked quite normal to him but he knew they weren't. Somehow the figures for extra fuel picked up had been spread amongst the entire fleet so nothing looked out of the ordinary.

That was easily stopped.

Typing out a memo for Paul to give his drivers, it told them that they would be getting a book of daily worksheets to complete, giving all the relevant info such as the driver's name, date, vehicle reg, trailer number, destination, start-mileage, end mileage, hours worked, fuel picked-up, and all the receipts for it.

Each page in the book was self-duplicating. One for the office and one to stay in the book for the driver. The journeys and their mileages could then be checked carefully. Jack knew he could examine the tacho's later on the pretence that the boss had asked him to do a check before the Ministry of Transport people visited the company again. He knew Paul wouldn't mind.

He never did like extra work.

81

Although the passport photo was of Michelle, albeit a younger version, the passport was in a different name.

Looking round guiltily, Jack closed the passport quickly, popped it back into her handbag and carried the cases downstairs where he waited for her in the hall.

He heard a taxi pull up outside and Michelle bounced down the stairs, full of the joys of spring even though it was winter.

"Sure you've got everything?" he asked, trying to act normally.

She nodded.

The taxi driver collected her things and put them in the boot. Michelle looked at Jack, smiled, and kissed him.

"I've got your number, lover-boy, so I'll text you, OK?"

And just as she got into the taxi Jack gave her a kiss.

"See you when you get back from bonnie Scotland then, Helen."

*

In the street outside Declan's house that evening, Rachel got in her car and drove off, threading her way carefully between all the badly parked cars that were along it. Most of them were parked half on the road where their owners had left them. Others were on the path. Off-road vehicles, she called them.

Out of town she stopped in a lay-by to make a phone call.

"That you, Jack?" she asked.

"Yes," he replied, somewhat curious.

"You at home?"

Jack was wondering how she'd got his number. Another person he knew he hadn't given it to.

"Well, are you?" she demanded sharply.

"What?"

"At home. Aren't you listening?" she snapped.

"Er, yes, why?" he asked.

"Good. I'm coming to your place. Shan't be long so put the kettle on. I'll bring some fish and chips with me, OK?"

82

In order to cover the Christmas and New Year holiday period, Mr Adams had told both Paul and Jack to find a skeleton staff. It was quite a usual thing to do and Jack put a notice on the board in the office, asking for volunteers. His name was at the top. Where he'd worked in Bristol, it was usually those with no kids who volunteered.

However, not long after he'd put the notice up, Jack saw Steph standing in front of it sucking the end of her pen, looking at the almost empty sheet. He walked slowly across the office and stood silently behind her. She was adding her name below his and he couldn't understand why. She had three kids who were still young enough to know that Father Christmas was real.

He took a step closer.

"Want to talk to me about it, Steph?" he whispered, suggesting they went into his office.

She closed Jack's office door, put some files on his desk as if they were going to run through them and, pulling her chair up next to him, she looked as though she was going to burst into tears.

Jack waited. She sniffed.

"Rob's taking them to his mother's. Aviemore," she explained. "There's always plenty of snow up there so they'll have a great time."

"So why aren't you going with them?" Jack asked.

From the end of her sleeve Steph took a tissue and blew her nose on it, then stuffed it back up her sleeve again.

"She and I don't get on," she began, shaking her head and staring at the top of Jack's desk. "Never have."

She turned to face Jack.

"At our wedding reception she took me to one side. 'At least you're fuckin' white', she snarled."

That took Jack by surprise.

She gave him a brighter smile and looked at him.

"See you're still covering up what's left of that scar, Jack."

Without realising Jack immediately touched his cheek with a couple of fingers.

"Not as much as I used to though, Steph. It's almost disappeared so I don't bother too much now."

She nodded her head. Wondered how he'd got it.

"So where y'going to spend Christmas then, Steph?"

It was only a question, but she turned in her chair and gave him one big cheeky smile.

"Comin' to your place," she laughed. "Be with you after we finish on Christmas Day ... or even before."

Jack was stunned into silence. He hadn't meant it to be an invitation.

"Hope you can cook?" she continued.

But the look she got left her in doubt.

"Well, OK, I'll get the food, you get the booze," she ordered.

She was thinking about it and Jack could almost hear her going through every last detail. She moved her chair closer. He was boxed in. Didn't like it. Felt paralysed. Wasn't fear though. Just Steph's intimidating comments.

"And what'll we drink then?" she asked him more seriously.

For once in his life Jack didn't know what to say.

"Well, all I can say is I hope you get a good whisky for after dinner," she continued, looking at him.

It wasn't a question, more of a command; it'd better be or else.

"So what'll we do after dinner?"

Jack froze again. She nudged his arm.

"Only joking," she laughed.

He sighed and began to relax. However, it was far too soon.

"Hope you like a bloody good breakfast."

83

"Gov," Cassie began, "Greg and I went back to that place again a couple of nights ago. Reckon there's a small laboratory in there. Some of the papers we photographed are from a firm called Roger's. Only had time for a brief look round, just didn't add up."

"Thanks Cass," the Major replied. "I'll make some enquiries."

He was just about to put the phone down when Cassie started speaking again.

"Did I tell you Greg's been seeing that bloke you knew? Y'know, the one you said was one of your best ever field officers?"

The reply was instant.

"What, Jack bloody Mason?"

"The very same. Works for Roger's Transport too. He's their accounts manager."

There was a pause before the Major continued.

"Well, well, well. How bloody convenient. What's he know?"

"Not really sure, but he knows Helen and Pete now. She'd told him her name was Michelle, but Greg told me he found her passport."

She paused for a while when she heard the Major laughing.

"I'll meet him somewhere discreet. Have a chat. Get him back. Could do with someone like him on the inside again. Especially with him working at Roger's Transport."

84

Rachel didn't ring the bell, just knocked on the door. Jack had seen her park her car in front of his house from his kitchen window and rushed to let her in. Hoped no one saw her there. Especially Paul. Knew he might have wondered what was going on.

But before handing him the carrier-bag with their dinner in it, Rachel put one arm round his neck and kissed him, tenderly at first, then harder when she pushed him back against the wall near the stairs in the hallway. The house-keys hanging on the wall rattled above Jack's head.

Jack was taken by surprise and although she'd teased him in the pub, he wanted to be alone with her. Even if she did carry a weapon. There in his home he felt comfortable to perhaps talk and learn, in a round-about way, if she were the same woman he'd followed on the train in Holborn.

Rachel's kiss, however, seemed to last ages and when they parted, she quickly passed him the carrier-bag that the fish and chips were in and asked him where the loo was. He pointed upstairs, moved into the kitchen, and began to put the meals on plates.

Minutes later, after hearing the flush go, he found Rachel was standing behind him with a sexy smile on her face. He put the plates on trays with the knives and forks and asked if she wanted any salt and vinegar. The shake of her head said 'no thanks'. Then, she swapped the knife and fork over to the other side and shook her head at him as if he should have known better.

"Coffee?" he asked.

She didn't reply until they were in the lounge with the trays on their knees.

"Got any wine?" she asked.

"Red or white?"

She picked a chip up in her fingers and began to eat it.

"Red if that's OK, Jack," she replied.

He put his tray on the floor, opened a bottle of red wine, and filled their glasses, handing one to her. She smiled as he lifted his tray off the floor and sat back on the sofa to eat his dinner.

"So what's all this about, Raich? And not only that, where d'you get my phone number from?"

She put her fork down and looked at him.

"If I told you that I'd have to kill you," she joked, but from the tone of her voice and the way she was holding her knife he began to wonder if she really would.

After dinner, Jack excused himself and went to the loo whereupon Rachel swiftly moved into the hall for a few seconds before coming back into the lounge. She sat down on the sofa again, waiting for Jack to come down.

"So what did you want then, Raich?" he asked as he was sitting down.

"Just wanted to see what your place was like," she lied.

She laughed and got up to go. But what she didn't tell him was she also wanted to look around his house, see if there were any photos from his past.

"Hang on, Raich," he moaned. "Where exactly *did* you get my mobile number from?"

She walked across the room to him, gently hung her arms over his shoulders and stared into his eyes.

"You called Paul the other day. Remember? And I asked you to let me know next time you were taking a bath."

Her lips gently touched the end of his nose.

"I can run it for you now if you like?" she purred.

But before Jack could say yes, she giggled, picked up her bag, collected her coat, and left. However, after she'd gone, he went into the hall, took the keys from the hook, and went onto the patio.

With a swift movement he flung them into the canal.

85

A couple of days after Helen had gone to Ullapool Jack had had a text from her, telling him she'd arrived there safely even though the car she'd hired wasn't what she'd asked for. After that, he didn't hear anything else from her. He even sent some texts, but she never replied. It was the twentieth of December and Jack was wondering now why she'd not text back.

In the pub, Pete was still doing a crossword, drinking his pint, and watching Rachel as she walked over to Jack, but he was now smiling, knowing that Jack was on his side. He nodded his head slowly. No one would have seen it. Jack frowned at him, asking 'what?', but Pete drank his pint and continued doing his crossword.

Christmas decorations hung from every possible place. Had been since just after bonfire night. A huge Christmas Tree stood in the main entrance and a smaller one was situated in the restaurant area. That one had an assortment of various-sized bright-coloured empty boxes under it which the local kids picked up and shook to see if anything interesting might fall out of them. Christmas music was playing through the pub's speaker system and in Jack's corner the log fire was blazing, spitting sparks out everywhere.

"So where's Michelle these days?" Rachel wanted to know as she stood warming her bum in front of the fire.

"Disappeared out of your life now, has she?" she added with generous helpings of sarcasm.

He'd not said anything to her about her going to Scotland and, sipping his pint, he motioned Rachel to sit down facing him.

"She's at her Mum's in Scotland for a while," he said glumly.

A look of amazement crossed Rachel's face, but it quickly dissolved and was replaced with a naughty smile.

"So you're on your own then?"

Jack took another mouthful of lager and nodded his head.

"Oh, poor you," she said, mocking him. "When does she get back?"

He moved his chair further away from the fire. His legs were getting too warm.

"Just before or after Christmas," he said, hoping it might be before.

"Well," she smiled, "at least you might still be able to share your Christmas dinner together eh?"

He nodded, smiling at the thought.

"Of course I could always take her place if she doesn't get back in time," she offered cheekily.

Jack almost spat his drink over the table.

"What you and me?"

"And why not?" she asked, pulling a face. "Bet you'd like some real female company over Christmas, wouldn't you?"

"And what would Paul say?"

"Him? He's bloody working."

"Yeah, well, so am I," Jack said, now sounding totally pissed off.

She thought for a while.

"Didn't think *you'd* have to."

Jack sighed.

"The girls in my office have kids, Raich," he told her.

He did think that going out with her would have been great, thinking about the night she'd brought the fish and chips to his place. He'd wanted that to happen ever since they'd first met, especially after their recent conversation regarding a bath, but learning who she was made him think twice.

The subject changed and she asked Jack how long he'd really lived there. He thought he'd told her that when they first met so, lying, he said it must have been about four or five years and asked why.

"Oh, it's nothing," Rachel said casually. "I was thinking the other night that we'd met somewhere else but ..."

"But what, Raich?" Jack shot back, curious to know. Reckoned she was digging a bit too deep. Asking the wrong questions.

Then Paul came in the pub and saved the day.

"Hi Jack," he said, unbuttoning his coat as he sat down next to them.

Jack laughed and told him never to say that on a plane. Paul only nodded.

He gave Rachel a frosty smile though and when she got up to go to the loo, he leaned closer to Jack.

"Can I see you in the morning, mate? Got to change some of my personal details."

Jack looked surprised. *Change some of his details?* Wondered what it was about.

"No probs, Paul," he replied, not wishing to ask anything else about it.

"Cheers Jack."

By the time Rachel returned, Paul had bought them another drink, but he then stood up, said something to her and made an excuse to go, so before he left them, they raised their glasses and thanked him for the drink.

Not long after he'd gone, and Rachel had sat down next to Jack, a ginger-haired bloke came in and stood at the bar. Rachel saw him.

He flicked his head towards the pub's doors and she frowned, suddenly announcing that she had to go.

Jack watched them leave. Saw Pete leave too, so he finished his pint and walked back home.

By the time he got home, flurries of snow were blowing thick and fast. Felt like Christmas was already there. He opened the front door and locked it after switching the hall light on.

He'd only just sat down with a large glass of whisky when his mobile lit up. He read the text.

It was the best news he'd had for a while.

86

"That bloody woman!" shouted Sir David down the phone. "She's been talking to the Irish Prime Minister about having some of our former soldiers tried over here for what she called 'war crimes during those troubled times', her words, and then she told him the chancellor would let his country have twenty million bloody pounds to help their economy! It's not hers, dam it!"

Geoff listened, shaking his head in disgust whilst Sir David told him more.

"Can't we put something in the bitch's tea?" he joked. "There are certain substances that can't be traced, y'know?"

Sir David sniggered.

"It's a good idea, Geoff, but we'd have to be very careful. Her old man's of Irish descent, so they might suspect something. She's trying her best to promote good relations over there. Most likely wants the Nobel Peace prize or even a peerage for Heaven's sake. The public aren't daft. They're all too well aware of what her motives are, and I don't think she realises it either. She's so up her own backside! At this rate the opposition could win the next election. And then what? She's supposed to our bloody Prime Minister!"

Sir David relaxed. Rant over.

"Also got a very discreet photo of that Rachel woman talking to the Irish PM. Alarm bells are ringing, Geoff!"

"Mmmm. We could always set up an accident for our own PM. After all, there are countless numbers of people we could blame."

Sir David chuckled at the suggestion and thought about it whilst dipping a biscuit into his coffee.

87

Christmas was coming up fast. Jack didn't say anything about it to Steph. Still called Helen by the other name when he was with her in the office, but Helen had told him that she wouldn't be there for Christmas which left Jack wondering if Steph would actually join him after work on Christmas Day instead.

He thought for a moment and decided to phone the pub. Ask Russ to reserve a table for two on Christmas Day. Just in case.

When he got through, Russ gave him the details of what was on the menu, but Jack told him he'd be in later and then he could pay him after deciding what he'd be eating. Russ explained that the kitchen was closing at five on Christmas Day, but Jack knew he'd be back home from work quite some time before that.

In the office the light on Jack's phone flashed on and off. Internal call. He picked it up.

"Jack, it's Paul. You free?"

Jack then remembered Paul had wanted to see him about the change of details.

"Yes mate," he said. "Come on up."

He put the phone down and, whilst he waited for Paul to arrive, he drew the blinds down so the others would know that he was not to be interrupted.

Jack looked through the door and signalled to Steph to bring two mugs of coffee in. Please, he added. She smiled and pulling a funny face, she gave him a curtsey.

She knew the signs. The blinds were down. That meant a visitor.

Paul and Steph crossed the outer office together and she let Paul go ahead before placing the coffees on Jack's desk. He nodded thanks and she closed the door, leaving them to whatever the meeting was about.

"Fuck me, Jack, you wouldn't have got this treatment downstairs," he joked. "Nice-looking woman, isn't she? Nice bum as well, eh?"

Jack knew where he was coming from. Saw him smirking. Agreed with him too.

"So what d'you want to see me about then, Paul?"

He picked his mug up and sipped some of his coffee.

"Well, I've got a different address now," he began and grinned like he was the cat that had got the cream.

Jack turned around to the cabinet behind him and opened the top drawer which contained all the employees' personal files, but Paul's wasn't there.

He remembered the old man had it. Wanted to look through it, didn't he? Jack quickly fished out a sheet of A4 that he always kept at the front of the drawers. Just in case.

Pencil in hand Jack waited to hear what Paul's new address was going to be. Also wondered if he'd mention being in a relationship as well. Hadn't before.

Paul put his mug down.

"I've left Rachel," he suddenly blurted out.

Jack looked shocked. He and Steph had long since suspected that something wasn't going smoothly after she'd seen Rachel with another bloke.

"Oh," Jack said, feigning surprise. "Sorry to hear about that, mate."

And Paul began to tell Jack where he'd moved to, but all the time he was writing, he was trying to think where Paul's new place actually was. He hadn't heard of the road. Thought it must be a new-build.

Paul started to tell Jack what had happened, but he knew it wasn't true, well not all of it, because he blamed it all on Rachel. It was s*he* who was having the affair, he said.

Jack supposed he was right to some extent, after all, hadn't she enjoyed those kisses at his place? He smiled to himself.

Paul finished his coffee, said thanks, and left Jack's office, eyeing up the other women on his way out.

As soon as he'd gone though, Steph rushed in, undid the blinds, and slowly gathered up the empty mugs on his desk. Her face was asking for an info update.

So when Jack told her she whistled.

"Told you she was up to no good, didn't I?"

Jack had to agree with her too and thought perhaps she'd got a nose for stuff like that. Hoped so anyway. Might be of some help one day.

She left the office and went back to look through the payroll that was going to be sent the next day. And as Jack sat there brooding, wondering when his friend Geoff would contact him, Steph was looking at him from the other side of the office.

Jack frowned.

She walked over and stood in the doorway, leaning against it. Her right hand was high up the door-jambe, above her head. She adjusted the weight of her size-14 body onto her left foot and placed her free hand on her hip.

"So, are we still on for Christmas Day then, Jack?"

"Cass, I've had it on good authority," Major Shaw began, "that our so-called mill was indeed used as a laboratory. Only a small one. A cave was dug out at the back of the mill. Second World War research establishment. Chemical weapons, that sort of thing. Top secret too. Supposed to have been cleaned up though before the Ministry sold it."

Cassie whistled long and slow.

"So how come it's still being used then, Gov?"

"Well, the story is that one of the blokes who worked there knew about it coming up for sale. The guy evidently had a grudge about something, so he filled out the appropriate paperwork that led everyone at the top to believe that the place had been officially and completely decontaminated. The man disappeared off the face of the earth after that, but now, since the confounded place has been, shall we say, re-discovered, all hell's been let loose and we're trying to find out where he might have gone."

"Any names then, Gov?"

"Not really, Cass, but lots of people have been burning the midnight oil and a couple of days ago someone came up with the name of an old scientist. Dead now though."

"Aw, that's a shame," she said.

"Bloody wasn't!" the Major barked. "Bastard blew himself to pieces when a bomb he was making for his Irish friends went off in his hands!"

In the pub that night, Jack filled out his reservation form for two dinners on Christmas Day. He told Russ it'd be for about 2 p.m. and that they'd have the prawn cocktail for starters, roast turkey and trimmings for the main and Christmas pudding with custard for dessert. Probably a bottle of bubbly or two as well. He paid and Russ asked who the lucky lady was. Told him he hadn't a clue, but there would be someone with him and hopefully yes, it would be a female. That made Russ laugh and Jack went to sit in his usual seat in the corner by one of the roaring log-fires.

He threw his short but thick winter-coat over the back of the chair and was just about to open his packet of crisps and take a sip of his pint when in walked Rachel.

She got her drink and headed straight over to where he was sitting.

"Hello you," she said. "Still on your own then?"

He nodded back, trying to smile.

She stood there for a moment. Her coat was in one hand, her wine in the other. She was wearing a white long-sleeved jumper that was almost skin-tight, as were her jeans. Jack wanted to tell her how fit she looked, but it would have been wasted. From the way she was standing she knew that already.

"What's up, Jack? Y'look as though you haven't seen a woman before."

He hadn't realised he was gawping at her like that and stopped.

"Y'sitting down then or are you going to stand there looking more desirable every bloody second?"

She giggled naughtily as she draped her coat over the back of the chair and sat down facing him. Her eyes stared into his as though she were trying to see what he was thinking. Femme fatale.

"You know what *you* want, Jack."

It was a statement of advice; a suggestion that she hoped would perhaps make him feel better.

He took another mouthful of his pint.

"And what's that then, Raich?" he asked, wiping his mouth on his sleeve.

"Oh, c'mon," she teased, "you know very well what I'm talking about."

He offered her a crisp and with that, a night of heavy drinking and flirting began.

Having been up to the bar several times Jack bought more drinks and Rachel asked if she could walk home with him again. At the same time her foot was stroking his leg and Jack was enjoying every bit of her attention, even though he was thinking about his relationship with Helen. But he wanted information about Rachel's friends, no matter what he had to sacrifice to get it.

A couple of drinks later and Rachel looked at her watch. It was almost 11 p.m.

"Shall we go now, Jack?" she asked impatiently. "It's getting late y'know."

He nodded, wondering why she wanted to go just then. Was she planning something? he wondered.

He held her coat out for her as she fed her arms into its sleeves, but she turned before he'd let go of her coat, causing one of his hands to brush lightly over her breasts. She quickly grabbed his hand as if to move it, but she didn't. Instead she held there for several seconds, letting him see that she was not displeased.

"Mmmm," she whispered. "See I'll have to keep my eye on you, y'naughty boy."

And winking at him she pushed her body close against his, pecking Jack on his cheek before they left the pub.

Some twenty minutes later and they were at Jack's front door.

"Coming in for a drink again then, Raich?"

Her smile said of course, and he opened the door, letting her go in first.

But when he switched the hall lights on Rachel was faced with something that she hadn't expected.

90

Rachel's eyes were glued to the back of Jack's black fleece that was hanging over the handrail at the bottom of the stairs. Couldn't take her eyes off it. Making her feel very startled were the three large yellow capital letters that were across the back of the fleece.

Couldn't have been clearer. Couldn't have been more intimidating. And, for Rachel, it couldn't have been more dangerous. The large yellow letters were staring right back at her and they were obviously causing concern.

Jack noticed the panic in her eyes and smiled to himself. Then, pretending to quickly conceal the three yellow letters, as if the fleece were the real thing, and he was one of the guys from the Farm at Langley, near Yorktown, Virginia, USA, where men and women joining the CIA are trained, he quickly turned the fleece inside out and pushed it into the space under the stairs.

He'd seen the horror on her face. Seen the colour suddenly drain from it. But he only wanted to tease her, see what she'd say or do. He waited but there was no response for what seemed a long time.

"Oh God!" she shouted. "You're not with them, are you?"

He noticed she'd clenched her fists.

"And if I were, Raich?"

She thought for a while before recomposing herself.

"Suppose you'd be even more interesting than you are at the moment."

"Hadn't occurred to me that I was," he told her.

She moved closer to him and placed her arms over his shoulders.

"Oh but you are, Jack," she whispered. "You're very interesting."

It was then that Jack decided to let her see the fleece more closely.

He pulled away from Rachel's arms and got it out from under the stairs then he threw it to her.

She held it out in front of her and read what it said, but she wasn't doing a very good job of concealing her anger.

What she hadn't seen before was the tiny writing that was between the three letters and Jack saw the fear in her build then subside and change into a huge sigh of relief. She spat the words out angrily. One by one.

"Culinary . . . Institute . . . of . . . America. You fucking bastard!"

She laughed but she knew Jack had caught her completely off guard. It was so obvious to Jack that he had to stop himself laughing as well. He knew how dangerous she might be. Knew he was going to have be extra careful.

"Great, isn't it?" he joked, but by the time he'd switched the hall light off and hung the fleece up again Rachel had become her smiling self and her lips were pressing hard against his. What's more, her hands were undoing buttons.

"Forget the bloody drink, Jack," she said, panting like she'd just finished running a marathon. So he did. And the kisses didn't stop.

But whilst Jack's eyes were closed tight Rachel nuzzled his ears, kissed his eyelids, kissed his neck, and poured loving kisses all over his face, smothering it. And all the time she was kissing him Jack knew what she was searching for.

It must have been nearly two in the morning when he unlocked the door and waved cheerio as Rachel got in a taxi to go home.

He got into bed, wondering why he'd let her go so far. Seconds later though he was thinking how enjoyable it had all been.

He was just leaning over to switch the bedside light off when his mobile started dancing about.

A text.

He read it.

'Jack Mason!!! That was Paul's partner. I'm ashamed of you!!!'

Jack laughed because there were lots of kisses after the text plus a crying face. He sent a text back.

'Cheers Steph. Caught me out again lol xxx'

'Huh, you never ask me to come back with you, though, do you?'

No kisses this time.

'You'd only be disappointed, Steph.'

'Let me be the judge of that!'

91

Jack got the blackest look from Steph he'd ever seen. Didn't even say good morning. And it wasn't until about eleven that she brought him his first a mug of coffee. Just plonked it down, spilling some of it all over his desk. Probably on purpose.

She walked away to leave him to clear the mess up, but when she sat down, she looked over at him and shook her head in disgust. Then she began to smirk and it eventually changed slowly to one of her lovelier smiles. Minutes later she rushed in carrying the payroll that Jack had to send.

She sat down and waited until he'd keyed in the code to send the BACS.

"You're a randy old bugger, aren't you," she chortled. "Hope she enjoyed it, lucky cow!"

And once the warbling noise on the phone had ended, they knew the weekly wages had been sent to the bank, letting Steph return to her desk to print off the wage slips.

The Thursday routine.

The list for volunteers over Christmas/New Year was still only two – Steph and Jack – but that was enough. Two of the girls were pregnant and the other had booked some time off to go on holiday somewhere warm with her partner. Jack didn't mind. There wouldn't be *that* much work to do.

At the end of the day Steph went in to see him.

"Can I ask you something, Jack?"

"Go on."

She fiddled about with her pencil in her hands.

"Just wondering what you're doing tonight?" she asked sheepishly.

"Eh?"

She looked at Jack and tilted her head on one side.

"Got to talk to you," she replied quietly. "Secret."

He had a sneaky suspicion there was more to it than that.

"OK," he told her. "Where we going to go?"

She suddenly burst out laughing.

"Not we, y'narna," she exclaimed. "Me!"

"Eh?"

"Me," she said, stabbing Jack's arm with her pencil. "I'm coming to yours tonight. Six-fuckin'-thirty so be ready!"

Jack was flabbergasted.

She chuckled as she went out.

"And be there!"

92

"And?"

Although the word was only three letters long, its pronunciation had lasted quite some time as the sound of it rose higher in pitch.

Rachel nodded her head then poured more wine into their glasses.

"Got a good close up of his face."

"And was there a scar on it?"

Rachel nodded slowly.

"And what did it look like?"

She put her glass down on the table and looked into Declan's green eyes.

"It was just a scar, very faint but it looked like it might have been caused by something round," she said.

"Hmmm. I wonder?"

"How did you know though?"

He sighed.

"Connor was wearing a ring on his left hand. His initials were raised on the ring. When he smashed him in the face it left the scar. He's left-handed, that's why the mark's on his right cheek."

Rachel loaded her fork with some food and put it in her mouth whilst Declan drank his wine and topped his glass up.

"How come you didn't see it before then?" he asked.

But she didn't tell him. Couldn't.

"Evidently covered it up with make-up," she said, knowing it wasn't a lie.

"Clever bastard! Wonder who advised him to do that then eh?"

She shrugged her shoulders.

"So what now then?" she asked.

Declan put his glass down and leaned in his chair, pushing it back until it was rocking on two legs. Rachel eyed him cautiously, waiting for him to go too far and fall over.

"I'll get word to Brendan that we've found him, but I reckon *you* should just forget about him."

"You said they were moving Brendan soon though, Dec."

"Yep, they are," he laughed.

"What y'laughing at?"

"He's going to up the road. Stafford!"

93

Throughout the day at work, Steph had been glancing at Jack more than usual and the glances were asking too many questions.

He signalled for her to come in his office and he didn't look pleased.

"Now what's all this nonsense about you coming to my place tonight then?" he asked, raising his voice.

She frowned. Wasn't used to hearing Jack like that.

"Well?" he demanded, wanting an answer.

She gulped.

"Just thought your place would be perfect for what I have to tell you."

She couldn't understand why Jack was being so strange to her. He gave her a very serious look then reached into the bottom drawer of his desk and got a tissue for her.

And that's when he gave the game away.

Her hand suddenly clipped the back of Jack's head. She'd heard him chuckling and seen his shoulders moving when he leant into the drawer.

"You bloody sod!" she shouted and began laughing whilst thumping his arm. "Thought I was in bloody trouble!"

God knows what the other girls in the office were thinking.

"I'll be ready at half-six, Steph," he told her, "but no hanky-panky OK?"

She threw him a look.

"What meeeeee?"

"Yes you," he snapped, and before he could say anything else, she flung her arms round him and gave him a big silly kiss.

"See you later," she whispered and walked out of the office, leaving the door open.

Jack got up and undid the blinds. The other girls were staring across the room wondering what the hell had been going on.

94

At home, Jack had just taken a shower and hung his suit on its hanger. He threw a shirt and some jeans on. Couldn't understand why Steph had wanted to talk to him at his place. Didn't know what it could possibly be about.

She rang the doorbell at 6.45 p.m. and waited for Jack to open it. He heard the taxi drive away. He was looking at his watch, about to tell her she was late, but he didn't get the chance. She barged straight passed him and stood in the hallway.

"Come on then, get the kettle on, I'm bloody freezing!"

It was too.

The wind from the north-east was bitter and Jack quickly closed the door. Snow was expected that night. The weather girl on TV had not long since said so.

Steph looked him up and down, and tutted.

"Good bloody job I didn't get dressed up then eh?"

"Want something in your coffee?" Jack offered, not taking any notice of what she was moaning about.

"What y'got?"

"Whisky."

She stood there thinking, then, he led her into the lounge.

"What sort?"

"What would you like? Blend or a malt?"

She looked at him and smiled.

"You choose," she said quietly and sat herself down on the sofa.

Jack went back into the kitchen and returned with a bottle of

Talisker and two glasses, but no coffee.

He poured hers first and passed it to her. She held her nose over it, taking in its rich peaty aroma whilst Jack poured one for himself.

"Cheers," he said, raising his glass.

They touched and Jack sat down in one of the armchairs, facing her.

"So what did you want to chat about?"

"It probably doesn't mean anything to you, Jack," Steph began, "but my old man's been telling me that he often sees some of our vehicles when he's on the road at night. He's a driver too, y'know."

Jack leaned forward a little. One elbow on his thigh. One hand covering his mouth.

"Go on," he said slowly.

"Well, he reckons there's a deal going on."

"How d'you mean?"

"He told me that he's often seen one of our vehicles, a rigid I think it's called, in a lay-by with one of its curtains pulled back a bit. A transit van plus a couple of guys were looking as though they'd been loading stuff from it into the van or from the van into the lorry."

Jack stood up and poured some more whisky into her glass.

"Steph, that's probably to do with that meeting I had with the boss," he exclaimed. "Someone's been fiddling the fuel figures and hiding them in the other vehicles' paperwork. Trouble was our supplier is an old friend of Roger's and the bill we used to get was for the entire fleet, so we never got to see which vehicle was picking up more fuel if you see what I mean."

Steph looked gone out at him.

Jack told her they'd already started monitoring the fuel pick-ups and that he suspected that someone at the garage might be involved as well.

"What you're telling me is probably about some of the wine that's going missing," Jack finally said.

She looked shocked.

"The police have been told but we've nothing as yet to go on. It's never the stuff we pick up from Amazon though. Have to be bloody careful with them. They give us tons of work. But we could lose other contracts if we're not careful."

She put her drink down on the small coffee table next to her.

"Bloody hell Jack. Never knew about that. But doesn't Paul do the wine run for that cheap booze place?"

He sighed deeply.

"Well, I'll talk to Roger about it, Steph. That's also a bloody good contract. Not very big, but it's steady work and it pays well too."

Steph's mouth dropped open, saw Jack looking at her, and eventually closed it.

"Well, Rob didn't want to get anyone into trouble to start with, but only last week he said he saw it again. Said it was the third time he'd seen it. And it took place in the same lay-by. Along one of the smaller roads he goes down. And from what he said he saw last time, they were shifting some other things. Long sacks. Rob said they looked like weapons."

Jack's mouth opened wide.

"Whereabouts was this, Steph, did Rob tell you?"

She nodded and gulped some of her whisky.

"Not that far from here actually. In a lay-by along the A519 near Millmeece. I'll show you on that map we have in the office."

Jack moved over to her, sat down next to her, and gave her a very big cuddle.

"What's that for?" she muttered, but before he could tell her she

192

kissed him.

Jack gently pushed her away from him and told her that her husband wouldn't like what she wanted to do. She smiled sadly, agreeing with him and a few minutes later she headed off back home in a taxi.

Jack poured himself some more whisky. The police would have to be informed. Roger would have to be told as well. And no doubt Rob would be interviewed about it too.

After going upstairs to bed, just as he was getting undressed, his mobile lit up.

A text.

'Have you next time then xxx'

95

It was Christmas Eve and Jack hadn't seen or heard anything from Helen. He knew then she wouldn't be spending Christmas with him. He began to wonder where she was and what she was doing.

The police had been informed about what Steph's husband had told her and they were having a word in the boss's office. They were also going to have a quiet word with Rob too.

The office that day was otherwise empty apart from Steph and Jack. He'd let the others go early, knowing they would no doubt be getting ready for the big day tomorrow.

He meandered over to Steph's desk with his mug of coffee and sat down next to her. No point sitting in his office on his own.

"Never realised you didn't want to carry on the other night, Jack," she said quietly as she gently laid her hand on his arm. "Wasn't expecting a refusal. Would have got four points for that at a horse show, wouldn't I?"

Jack shook his head and smiled at her.

"You wouldn't have known what to do with them though, Steph."

They laughed.

"Felt a bit hurt too," she added solemnly.

They looked at each other.

"Thought you were only joking about it though, Steph, sorry," he replied. "Not getting it at home?"

She giggled in her own sweet way. Naughty, but nice.

"Not as much as I'd like," she replied. "But you can relax a bit now though because I won't be round tomorrow."

Jack asked why not.

"I know you're expecting company, Jack."

She winked.

He told her he'd not heard anything from 'that tart' and she laughed.

"Probably knows what a two-timing bugger you really are eh?"

He laughed and took another sip of the coffee that Steph had made.

The main office phone went off and Steph got up to answer it. Jack saw her mouth 'it's for you' and waited for her to put the call through to his office.

"Jack, it's me."

"At last!" he shouted.

"Piss off Jack!" she hissed. "I've got to go back home to my Mum's again."

There was sadness in her voice and Jack asked her what had happened. She didn't answer straight away, but eventually she informed him that her Mum had passed away. Happened a few days ago, she told him.

Jack felt sad for her. Knew what she must be going through.

"Well love," he said, "just let me know when you'll be coming back, please."

"OK Jack, but it'll be a while because of all the things I'll have to sort out," she told him. "Y'know, funeral, will, tell the people renting her old house it'll be on the market etc. Y'know how it is."

"Ok Michelle," he said, "I'm so sorry."

He paused. A little respect. A remembrance.

"Have missed you though," he told her eventually.

There was a short laugh.

"Yeah, I bet you bloody have. Bye."

Steph had been listening and during their conversation she'd been making faces.

"You're a smooth-talking little shit, aren't you! Nearly had to find the bloody sick-bucket."

And she pretended to heave into her bin. Evidently done it before as well, because the noises were spot on. Signs of a misspent youth.

Steph came back to Jack's office with another mug of coffee. There wasn't much to do over the Christmas-New Year period apart from chat so that's what they did. And drink more coffee.

"Well, now that she's not going to be at yours for Christmas Dinner," she began, looking at him with a grin on her face, "how about we celebrate it on our own somewhere?"

So, he told her he'd already booked a table in the pub and was she interested?

She didn't say anything. Just gave him a look that asked if he was joking or not, but Jack nodded his head.

"What time's it booked for?" she asked, still not sure.

"About two-ish," he told her.

"You're serious, aren't you?" she said, frowning at him.

"Yes Steph, I am," he said licking his lips.

And he ran through what he'd ordered.

"OK?"

"What we drinking then?"

"Bubbly!" he replied. "Still coming then?"

The smile grew larger and larger across her face.

"How many?"

"A couple."

"I'd better be careful then."

"What d'you mean by that?"

She kissed Jack's cheek and picked up her mug.

"Well, I might just have to get naughty this time."

96

"So when're they moving him, Dec?"

His face lit up, showing his white teeth, not perfect but still there.

"After Christmas but before the New Year, why?"

"I was wondering if he'd like a 'welcome to your new home' card, that was all."

Declan laughed and he pulled Rachel to him, kissing her hard.

"He'd probably love *that,* knowing him. Once he's settled in though, we'll be able to get on with what he was planning to do, eh?"

Rachel nodded.

"Will it be very dangerous?" she asked, wondering what Dec and Michael had been doing.

"That depends if he wants us to be part of it. I've heard he now wants to finish that bloke off, but I think he'll get someone else to do it. He doesn't like using family if he can avoid it, and there's loads of rough buggers who'd do it for peanuts."

Rachel frowned.

"You only get monkeys with peanuts, Dec."

He smiled at her and nodded his head.

"Yeah I know, but we won't be involved with his murder, will we? Keeps us in the clear then, eh?"

"Would he pay much though?" she wanted to know.

Declan shook his head and grinned.

"Nah! Couple of hundred quid or so."

"That's not anywhere near enough for a contract-hit, the tight bastard! I wouldn't trust them, Dec."

97

Christmas Day arrived and the moment Jack got into the office he was smothered in kisses. Steph had been waiting for him, wearing a hat with a large sprig of mistletoe sticking out of it.

Christmas greetings out of the way, she looked at him. Curiosity was written across her face.

Hands on hips she demanded, "So where is it then?"

"What?" Jack snapped back.

"My bloody present," she hissed, then, "You're horrible you are!"

Jack shook his head and smiled.

"Oh that," he began, "thought I'd give it to you when we have dinner later."

She eyed him carefully.

"You haven't got one, have you?"

And after she didn't get a reply, she stormed off downstairs. Didn't speak to him for an hour. Jack didn't mind though because it let him finish some work off. He had to prepare the wages for the few who were still working over the Christmas/New Year period.

It was just after two when they got to the pub. The tables in the restaurant were covered in Christmassy tablecloths and on each table was one of those pretend candles that light up when switched on. There were only fifteen tables set for dinner and they were spread out far enough away to help keep the customers' conversations more private.

Jack and Steph were shown to their table by one of the staff.

The drink came and they sipped the champagne slowly as they faced each other across the table. Christmas carols were being piped through the pub's speaker system. Kings College Cambridge. An exciting Christmas atmosphere surrounded them, and Steph was drinking it all in.

Whilst people at other tables were popping corks Jack and Steph wished each other a Merry Christmas. The sound of their champagne flutes touching and the emotional music brought a tear to Steph's eyes and, looking at Jack, she wiped them with her serviette. Seconds later, her face had lit up as they pulled the crackers that were on the table, with Jack insisting that they wore the hats throughout their meal.

Jack placed his glass on the table, fished about in his jacket pocket. Steph was watching his every move.

"Damn!" he whispered, loud enough for her to hear. "Where did I put it?"

Steph's face dropped to a look of disgust as Jack patted his pockets in turn, trying to find something. She was not amused.

"Ah," he said eventually, "found it."

And Jack passed a small gift-wrapped parcel over the table to her.

The only words that could describe her look were 'you sod'. She shook the box first and then began to untie the bow. The wrapping paper was carefully removed, folded up, and put on the table. She looked thoughtfully at the black box without reading what the name on it was.

She opened it.

"Wow Jack!" she cried. "This is beautiful!"

People in the room looked on as Steph got up, moved round the table, and planted a big kiss on Jack's face.

"Thank you, thank you, thank you," she shouted, almost in tears. "Can I put it on?"

Silly question really, but Jack said she could, and he looked on as she took the watch from its box and fastened it round her wrist. He reckoned the others in there thought he'd proposed or something because they all began to clap.

Steph was very happy and slightly embarrassed by all the attention she was now receiving. She mouthed a 'thank you' to them all and sat down. Only then was it that she read the name on the box.

She whistled and quietly said 'Seksy'. Then, she held the box in the air showing everyone what it was as though it was the most expensive Cartier watch in the world.

Some older women near to them nodded and smiled, bless. The younger ones wow'd and nudged their partners as if to say I wanted one of those, and Jack watched the guys' eyebrows raise up to meet in the middle. Got the feeling they wished he hadn't been there.

Each part of the dinner came and went, and in between, Steph, God bless her, kept raising her hand to look at the watch, tell Jack the time, then blow him a kiss.

"When's Rob back with the kids, Steph?" he asked, trying to make light conversation.

"Oh, er, not until about the third of January," she sighed. "He wished me a Merry Christmas before I went to work this morning, so did the kids. They were yelling about what Santa had brought them."

Subdued, she hung her head down and for one moment Jack thought she was going to cry. Instead, she raised her head and whispered something to him, but he didn't catch what it was and fired off a puzzled look.

They finished the last of the second bottle of bubbly and Steph looked at her new watch.

"It's nearly five," she told Jack. "Time to go."

Jack held Steph's coat as she put it on, and, thanking Russ for the delicious Christmas Dinner as they left, he put a tenner in the staff's

Christmas Box that was on the bar top.

"Merry Christmas mate," he said.

By the time they got home, Steph was giggling even though it was raining, and the cold north wind was freezing them both to bits. Jack's shoulder ached and he rubbed it before unlocking the door to go inside. Steph noticed but didn't ask what he'd done. She already knew about the scar on his cheek but not the nasty-looking ones.

She almost ripped her coat off and flung it over the chair in the kitchen when she got in and, kicking off her heels, she looked straight into Jack's eyes.

"Jack Mason," she said, kissing his lips after each word. "You. Are. One. Lovely. Fuckin'. Bloke."

Jack put his arms round her and gave her a hug. She tutted.

"Is that all?"

It wasn't.

He kissed her waiting mouth and felt her tongue slip between his lips, searching for something.

When he came up for air Jack asked if she'd like a whisky. He felt her head nod slowly against his shoulder and easing her away from him so he could open the bottle he poured some out for them. Then, they moved into the lounge.

She stood looking at the Christmas tree, such as it was, and asked Jack to stand next to her. He did and she took a selfie of them together.

"Won't Rob be angry if he sees that?" Jack asked her.

"I won't show it to him," she whispered and kissed him again.

They had a couple more glasses of whisky then she suddenly looked up at him.

"C'mon then, mister. I've got a Christmas present for you to undo."

98

Back at work after the Christmas/New Year break Jack had had no more messages from Helen. Couldn't understand why. After all, she was only at her Mum's, not the other side of the bloody world. And Steph had wound him up by telling him she'd got another guy somewhere.

On Saturday afternoon, he was hurrying down the road on his way home from doing some shopping. It'd been trying to snow again and between the flurries the sun had kept popping out for a few moments. With his head tucked into his shoulders Jack dodged people on the pavement, but halfway down the street, where the cars could park on that side of the road, he was suddenly aware of a flashing light at the end of the road. He stopped. Couldn't quite make out what it was. Watched for a few seconds as he walked on.

The sun's light was bouncing off a car's wing mirror, reflecting it towards him and as he moved nearer to the car he could see the car's mirror turning slowly, following him, keeping him in its view as he walked down the road.

But as he got nearer, the car suddenly drove off. And when it did, he saw the back of the head of the passenger.

It was Rachel.

He turned around to head back up the road, cursing himself for not spotting it sooner. He turned left and went straight into Iceland.

"Fancy meeting you in here, Mr Mason," said a very cheery voice and, turning around to make sure it was her, Jack came face to face with Steph. And her three kids. They started to giggle and hid behind their mum, but she pulled them in front of her and told them who Jack was. Heads down, looking guilty and murmuring to each other, they sounded like they were saying hello to one of their teachers.

She let them go and they ran down the aisle to the ice-cream freezer. Steph looked at him.

"What's up?" she asked quietly. "You look as though you've seen a bloody ghost."

He told her what he'd seen, and she told him to be careful.

"I'll text you when I get home, OK Jack?"

He was sure she was about to kiss him then realised where she was and who she was with, so she didn't. She smiled, squeezed his hand, and they parted, she darting across to her kids to stop them getting tons of ice-cream out of the freezer and Jack heading for the other door at the back of the store that went out into the car park near to where he lived.

As he crossed the car park, he kept looking for that old grey car. He hadn't even taken its registration number and cursed for having let his guard down.

Inside his house, Jack put away what shopping he'd got and sat down with a cup of coffee. Outside, through the patio windows, the flurries of snow were more frequent and once or twice they became so thick he couldn't even see the other side of the canal. What had happened down that road earlier in the afternoon gave him a funny feeling.

He was about to draw the curtains when his phone went off. Jack felt a sigh of relief when he saw Steph's name come up on the screen.

A text.

'Was that car you saw an old grey Ford?'

Jack text back as fast as his fingers would let him.

'Yes why?'

'Saw one going round the roundabout outside your place a couple of nights ago, but it went right round and back to the one at the other end of the road. Did it three times. Slowly.'

'Bugger!'

'Shall I come over for a couple of hours. Babysitter'll be here soon. Was going out. Rob's away overnight.'

'OK Steph, text me when you're outside please. And thanks xx'

99

"So that was him, was it?"

Rachel nodded her head and carried on eating the pizza that they'd taken back home.

"Thought you said he was a big bloke though."

Rachel put her knife down.

"What gave you that impression, Dec?"

"Just the way you described him that's all."

She laughed and picked her knife up to cut another slice.

"Not him," she told him, "he's nothing to worry about. Wouldn't say boo to a fuckin' goose!"

They ate their meal and went into the lounge.

"When's my stupid partner getting some more wine then?" she asked.

Dec poured them both a glass of red, handed one to her, and stood there looking at his as he swirled it round in his glass.

"He's collecting a few boxes from the drinks van this week sometime."

They raised their glasses.

"To good old Paul," he said.

100

In the pub Jack was enjoying another pint, sitting in his usual place in the corner by the log-fire, and he noticed that Pete was nowhere to be seen again. Hadn't been in since just before Christmas. Seemed strange not seeing him there. Strange not being in Helen's delightful company as well.

There weren't many people in the pub either that evening. Perhaps everyone was getting over the Christmas and New Year madness and couldn't afford to go out again for a while. The decorations had all been taken down and hidden away until next year. Made the place feel even more empty now.

Jack had had some news from Helen though, but it wasn't that good. She'd text to say she was taking a holiday. Needed one after what had happened to her Mum she'd said. Just for a week. Somewhere warm but she hadn't said where. She was going to text him when she got back. But he didn't believe her. He'd heard that before.

Rachel popped in for a drink and said hello, and over a glass of wine she told Jack she was off to Portugal. Another one going on holiday. Two bloody weeks. Getting away from the wretched weather, she said. *Lucky for some*, he thought. Didn't say who she was going with though. Wasn't Paul. He was still at work.

Rachel didn't stay long though, just had the one glass of wine, said cheerio, and kissed Jack's cheek as she left the table. He wondered then if Pete had gone away as well. Lots of people did that time of the year.

Jack was supposed to be meeting Steph at six and as he looked at the pub's clock on the wall above the bar, he began to feel that she too, for whatever reason, wasn't going to arrive either.

They'd spoken that afternoon about who'd been watching him in the car. It had touched a raw nerve when she'd told him she'd seen the old grey car passing his house a few times, but he'd laughed it off, only now it was once again playing on his mind. He'd also told Greg about it too.

Having finished his second pint, he was just about to leave when his phone started vibrating in his coat pocket.

A text.

'Sorry Jack I can't make it. My eldest has gone down with a bug. See you tomorrow xx'.

He sent a text back saying he was sorry, hoped her lad would be OK. Couldn't be helped. Don't worry about it.

He left the pub. It was just coming up to 7 p.m.

When he got home, he switched on the TV and was about to pour himself a large glass of whisky, but he was interrupted when the doorbell suddenly rang.

101

Over dinner, Roger and his wife, Denise, were entertaining Doug and his good lady Angela. They'd been chatting about their next game of golf and, when the brandy was passed round the table, Roger's wife looked at Doug's and flicked her head up.

"Reckon we'll go into the sitting-room, Angela, and leave them alone in the lounge. It'll only be golf talk again, won't it?"

Angela smiled, nodding her head, and following Denise they left the dining room.

"After what you told me about that girl's husband seeing a transfer being made, we interviewed him and I made some enquiries."

He sipped his brandy as Roger waited to hear what Doug was going to say.

"There appears to be a more serious side to it than you think, Roger," the Inspector began. "It's about that wine contract you have. Transpires that Mr Mason, your man in accounts, could be involved and may be in a lot of trouble."

Roger's face changed and he frowned, expecting the worst.

"Oh God not him as well," he huffed. "What's *he* been up to then?"

Doug laughed.

"Oh it's nothing like that, m'friend. On the contrary."

And he began to recount what had happened to Jack some years ago in Bristol. Roger couldn't believe what he was being told and sat back in his armchair, shaking his head.

"Bloody hell Doug, I never knew."

What he also didn't know was that he'd also been informed by people linked to the security services that Jack was working with them to help gain more intelligence about the old mill.

They lifted their glasses to their mouths and continued to talk about their next game of golf.

102

When Jack opened the front door, he was confronted by two large figures dressed head to toe in black. Over their heads Balaclavas hid their faces.

They man-handled him back inside. Didn't give him time to retaliate. Didn't get the chance to shout out because as they barged him back inside his house, one of the guys stuffed something large and round into his mouth. Taped it shut. Didn't get a good look at them either because his head had suddenly been covered with a sack, secured with duck-tape around his neck.

And Jack had never felt so afraid in his life.

A knee connected with his groin and he crumpled up on the floor, cursing, trying to cover himself in case he got more kicks, but one of the guys grabbed Jack's arms and pushed them behind him, strapping his wrists together.

Tight.

It jolted his shoulder and he let out a muffled scream. The other guy had tied his ankles together as well before pulling his shoes off.

Hauling him up, they dragged Jack outside and threw him into the back of a van that was parked up in front of his door, waiting for him with its doors wide open.

His head cracked against the edge of one of the doors and he could feel blood trickling down his face. He collapsed in a heap against the side of the van, bumping against some small cardboard boxes. Sounded like there were some bottles in them.

It had taken barely a couple of minutes and no one had spoken a word. *Very professional,* Jack thought. *Bloody dangerous too.* Reminded him of his past.

Jack's nerves were frayed. He heard the front door of his house slam shut at the same time as the van's doors were closed. Someone banged twice on the side of the van and it drove off.

It was freezing and damp inside and Jack was getting colder and colder. Apart from his underwear he only had a thin shirt, jeans, and socks on, and he was shivering. Normally when he was invited out with friends he dressed for the weather, but this was no invitation and these people were certainly not his friends!

Leaning against the boxes with his knees under him Jack began to cramp and, try as he did, he couldn't move his legs enough to stop the pain. He was thrown across the van whenever it went around any corners which stopped the cramps, but only for a few minutes. He had no idea which direction the van was taking him, but he had a good idea why.

He tried to visualise the route they were taking but they made too many turns and Jack became disorientated.

Eventually, the road seemed to straighten out and there were noises of other traffic too.

Next to him.

Going faster than him.

Thought they were on a motorway because the road seemed smooth, but whilst that was going through his mind he was having difficulty trying to keep warm. That was most important now. He was also getting very uncomfortable.

Jack decided to try and lay on his side so he could stretch his legs a bit. It worked for a while but then the van began to slow down very quickly, and the cardboard boxes squashed him against the back doors. The blood had stopped running down his face by then, but his head was still pounding.

At one point, Jack reckoned they were going through a town because they weren't going very fast. Kept stopping and starting as though they'd met a few sets of red lights.

Hadn't a clue.

The van drove on but the road noise was different again and there were some sharp bends which threw Jack about even more. There were lots of potholes too.

How long he'd been in the van only God and the devil knew. They slowed right down and bumped over what Jack thought was a railway-crossing, but this had a hump.

Jack's mind was thinking overtime. Couldn't be a crossing. Must have been a hump-backed bridge. That meant it must have been over a canal or a river then.

The van picked up speed but not by very much. Couldn't. Slush was hitting the wheel arches and a lot of it was leaking into the van, making him more wet. More miserable. More cold. And the boxes were also getting wet. And soft. So soft he could almost feel the bottles inside.

He suddenly lurched to the back of the van when it began climbing up a steep hill which twisted left and right as it went up. Then, when the van seemed to level out, it suddenly turned right, bumping over what felt like a very rough farm track.

And that was where the van stopped.

103

Jack's phone hadn't stopped ringing all night and Steph was getting more and more pissed off because he wasn't answering it, so by 10 p.m. she decided that he must be staying overnight somewhere. *Probably with another of his growing number of 'bitches'*, she thought.

"You're a rotten bastard, Jack!" she screamed as she put the phone down.

*

"Come on Jack. Pick it up. mate!"

Greg had also been trying to contact him as well. Since 8 p.m. And it was now getting on for eleven-fifteen.

Hadn't arranged to call him. Was just that something had come up. Needed to pass a message on urgently. Tell Jack what they'd discovered in the old mill's building.

*

Wet and freezing cold, Jack was now a very worried man. The van's engine was still running, and he heard someone get out. Only one person though.

One set of footsteps crunched on the snow as someone walked round to the back of the van and opened the doors. A howling blast of icy wind suddenly smashed into him, immediately chilling him to the bone. He shivered. Cold and afraid.

He was grabbed, hauled out of the van, and dropped on the ground. Smashed his nose when he hit it. Blood ran into his mouth through the tape that secured what Jack reckoned by then was a couple of pairs of old sweaty socks that had been stuffed there.

The van's doors slammed shut and Jack thought the guy was going away, but he didn't. A heavy boot found his shoulder and Jack cried out in pain when the stranger kicked him again and again. His tongue was out of the way under the socks inside his mouth. A kick to his face could have made him bite it in half.

A boot went into Jack's ribs a couple of times before another hit his face. Then it suddenly stopped.

And Jack waited.

He was trying to control his shivering. Trying to keep hold of his senses. And after a few minutes of unnerving silence, Jack heard a man's voice suddenly growl.

"Die y'bastard!"

104

The phone was ringing. It was eight o'clock. Declan opened his mobile, listened to the message and smiled as he put the phone back on the table.

Rachel looked at him.

"Who was it?" she enquired.

"Pat said they've just picked him up and he's in the van going to be taken care of somewhere. Said he'll let me know where later on."

Rachel smiled and crossed the room.

"Be glad when they get rid of him, Dec, then we can carry on with the other work. Still get the wine that my useless fuckin' partner gets though eh?"

Declan started to laugh.

"What's up?" she asked him.

"Just thinking," he said. "If only Mr Adams knew what was happening when he let Paul drive that Cut Price Booze's truck."

105

Jack's heart was beating faster and faster. Felt like it was going to burst any minute soon. He tensed up. Tried not to pee himself as he waited for whatever method his executioner was going use to dispatch him.

He started counting the seconds away.

One and.

Two and.

Three and.

Four and.

Four?

Nothing was happening.

The man just walked away to the front of the van, got in it, and, after turning it round, drove off.

Jack breathed a sigh of relief when he heard it going back down the steep hill, the same way they'd come.

He wept openly, thanking God and anyone else that was listening as every rigid muscle in his body suddenly relaxed. His bladder did too. At least it was warm. Adrenalin kicked in and he realised he had to move.

Fast!

Under the snow Jack's hands could feel the ice covering the large rocks that were in the frozen ground and he knew he had to free his wrists.

In the arctic wind, particles of ice were hitting his skin like small sharp needles and, although he was feeling rough, he somehow had to get his hands in front of him. So, wriggling about like a demented circus clown, he managed to pull his hands from behind his back, under his backside and feet.

He found a sharp-edged rock and began to saw through the rope that they'd tied him up with. The effort was making him feel warmer too, but he didn't want to sweat in case he froze. Jack knew he had to get away from that desolate place as soon as possible. Knew he could die out there in the cold.

The rope turned out to be thin binder-twine. *Not that professional then*, he told himself. This raised his hopes and made him smile.

The air was freezing and there was a smell of pine trees everywhere. He could hear them blowing in the wind.

Once his wrists were free, he yanked the sack off his head and spat out the socks. Gulped two huge breaths of the freezing air. Looked at the socks. Definitely two pairs. Definitely sweaty ones too.

And sitting on the frozen ground Jack began to undo his ankles. Took longer than he thought because his fingers were numb, but he managed it and stood up, moving around trying to get some warmth back into his badly bruised body.

Jumping up and down to get the circulation back, he began swinging his arms around like a mad man. Bugger the pain, he thought.

Then, he moved his head up, down, and in circles. Millions of stars twinkled in the night sky, through the light flurries of freezing snow and ice. He'd not seen so many since he'd been in the outskirts of Sarajevo many years before. The moon wasn't full, but its light illuminated the surrounding area and Jack realised he was on the top of a hill somewhere. Quite high up too.

On his left was woodland. Behind him the nose edge of a mountain reared up a thousand feet. To his right, the hill descended through rough moorland. A narrow road snaked down towards what looked like a large lake in the valley below.

And suddenly Jack shouted a very loud: 'YESSSSS!'

106

Picking up his mobile which was on the bedside table, Declan smiled as he listened. Rachel looked at him as she ran her fingers through the hair on his chest. He placed the phone back on the bedside table and turned to look at her.

"Well?" she asked, moving her hand further down Declan's body.

He jumped when her hand found what she was searching for.

"He's been taken care of, babe."

"What'll happen now then?"

"Haven't a clue, but I don't think we'll be seeing much of him."

And just before Declan pulled Rachel to him and kissed her, he moved one arm out of bed and switched off the light.

107

Jack knew exactly where he was. He'd walked over these hills more times than he liked to remember. Run over them too. Even carried very heavy Bergens on his back. These hills were almost a second home to him.

He was in the Brecons, at the top of the hill between Talybont-on-Usk and the Pentwyn Reservoir. Torpantau. He looked at his watch. It was just coming up to 11.40 p.m.

He picked up the small sack that had covered his head and put it on, wearing it like a hat, then he put both pairs of socks over his own and began to make his way down the steep hill.

The road was icy in places, but he didn't mind. At least he was getting warmer and in amongst the trees he knew he'd be partially sheltered from the arctic blast. The further he went down the hill the happier he became.

Estimating the distance to the nearest houses to be about five or six miles, Jack knew he'd have to get a move on. He went over the bridge at the bottom of the hill where a river ran under the road. A waterfall was further up to the left and was used by schools for adventure training, letting the kids go under the falls and then slide down into the pools. Good fun to some, absolute terror to others.

The road levelled out but there wasn't much shelter and the snow was falling heavily. It was deep, it covered his feet as he trudged on. Had to keep going.

Eventually, when a cottage came into view, Jack went up the lane to it and knocked hard on the door. Moments later, an outside light came on, almost blinding him and a guy about Jack's age appeared in the doorway, staring at him for a few seconds in disbelief.

"Bloody hell, man," he shouted suddenly, "don't stand there. Come in out of the cold for God's sake!"

Jack followed him inside. The guy looked him over suspiciously.

"So what've you been up to then?" he asked in his sing-songy Welsh accent as he looked at Jack's bloodied face, the wet patch around his thighs, and what clothes he was wearing.

"Stag-night prank," he lied.

The guy made a smile and put the kettle on.

"You look bloody freezing, man," he called from the kitchen. "Stupid prank if you ask me. You could've died out there dressed like that. Oh, I'm Bryn."

Tell me about it, Jack was thinking, and Bryn came back into the room with two mugs of hot sweet tea.

"Get that down you," he said, looking at Jack as if he were a doctor. He looked at Jack's face and passed him a wet cloth.

"Need to get your face cleaned up a bit too. You fall over then?"

Jack thanked him, and wiped his face, nodding as he held the mug of tea in one hand, feeling its warmth. He sipped it carefully. His lips were cut and swollen.

"I'm Jack. Jack Mason," he managed to say.

"Well Jack, I shouldn't think you've broken anything since you've managed to walk here, but I'll just check."

And Jack watched as Bryn gently pressed his hands over his ankles, legs, and then his arms. He pressed his shoulder, causing Jack to let out a cry. Bryn stopped and looked at him, but he told him it was from an old wound, an accident he'd been in.

So Bryn watched Jack as he drank more tea.

"Where've you got to get to then, Brecon?" he asked.

Jack shook his head and sighed.

"Afraid not," he said. "Rugeley."

Bryn put his mug down as his eyebrows knitted together.

"Where's that then?"

"Staffordshire," Jack told him.

Bryn looked at his watch.

"How you going to get there this time of the night?" he asked.

Jack also looked at his watch. It was just after one-fifteen.

"Can I use your phone please?" he asked.

Bryn nodded and gave his house phone to Jack.

Holding it for a few seconds he wondered who he could ring. He couldn't ring Helen because she was away. He thought about Rachel, but she was away. Couldn't remember Greg's number. Not then, so Jack tried another.

It rang for quite some time before it was answered and, explaining where he was as best he could, he heard the voice at the other end of the line ask for the postcode. He asked Bryn and repeated it to the person he was speaking to.

"I'll be there in about two or three hours then."

Jack smiled and handed Bryn's phone back to him, thanking him.

Bryn began to ask Jack what he did, and for the next hour or so, they chatted about their jobs. Turned out that Bryn worked for the Forestry Commission and knew the area like the back of his hand. Jack told him he knew the area very well too. Used to hike over the mountains, summer and winter, but that had been quite some time ago.

They drank more hot tea and chatted on about how beautiful the area was, even in winter. They exchanged names, addresses, and phone numbers because Jack wanted to visit him later and say a proper thank you for his hospitality. Probably get a good walk done together as well.

Before they knew it though, there was a loud knock on the door and they both looked at each other.

"Bet that'll be your lift then, Jack."

He nodded and got up, followed Bryn, and when he opened the door, Bryn laughed.

"Good morning. Like a cup of tea then?"

Steph shook her head.

"Thanks, but we have to get back."

She looked at Jack.

"Don't we?" she said sternly.

Nodding and saying thanks to Bryn for all he'd done they walked back through the snow to Steph's car which she'd turned around and parked at the end of Bryn's short lane. He waved, closed the door, and seconds later they were plunged into pitch darkness as Bryn switched off the cottage's outside light. The snow was falling heavily. Fist-sized snowflakes.

When he got in Steph handed him a tin of golden syrup.

"Get some of that down you."

He looked at her.

"Where d'you learn that?"

"Don't ask."

And just as Jack was settling himself in the car, about to stick the spoon into the syrup, he noticed two headlights coming slowly towards them through the snow and as it passed under one of the few streetlamps that was still on he suddenly recognised the car.

"Duck down and don't start the car!"

From the tone of his voice Steph knew he wasn't joking and hutched down in her seat, as low as she could, almost out of sight.

A car moved slowly passed them very carefully through the

deepening snow. Jack managed to look at the driver's face. It was concentrating, staring hard through the hypnotic snow that was hitting the windscreen, hands gripping the steering wheel, eyes trying to look through the windscreen beyond the wipers that were failing to move much of the snow away.

And eventually, the car's taillights disappeared from view.

Steph looked at him.

"What was that all about then?"

"That was Rachel!"

108

Jack's mobile was ringing. It was only 11 a.m.

"Hi Steph," his grumpy voice said.

"Just wondering how you are, Jack," she asked.

"Felt better," he grumbled as he got out of bed to go for a pee.

"The boss was wondering where you were, so I told him you'd rung in sick, OK?"

Jack was about to ask how she was, but the phone suddenly went dead. The boss had just come into the office.

Jack took a shower and went downstairs. He was feeling battered and bruised, thankful that he was still alive, and sitting in the kitchen he began to eat some breakfast. Just cereals and coffee. Black. Two cups. And as he was washing the dish up afterwards, he heard a loud banging on his front door.

His heart missed a beat and he held his breath for a few seconds, then he peered carefully through the gap in the kitchen curtains and into the dull grey morning. There were two people standing outside in the snow. Their car was parked in the open space in front of his house.

Jack went to the door and asked what they wanted. They showed him some ID. Plain-clothed police officers. He checked each one thoroughly and looking all around to make sure no one was watching, he asked them to come in.

"Mr Mason? Jack Mason?" one of them asked.

He nodded and sat down.

"We'd like you to come to the station with us if you would. Don't worry. You're not under arrest."

Well that's good news then, he told himself and they waited whilst he got the rest of his clothes on.

"Could you put the clothes you wore last night in this bag please sir?"

Sir? he liked that.

Jack collected them and carefully put them in the bag. Had an idea why the police wanted them. Forensics would have a field day.

Outside in the cold Jack almost slipped over in the icy snow. He was shivering by the time one of the officers opened the rear door, placing his hand over Jack's head as he got in the back. Once Jack's seat belt was fastened, they drove off.

Minutes later he was shown to a room. Fluorescent lights made it look very bright. The room was bare with just a table and four chairs in it. Jack had been looking round. A camera was in one corner, high up in the ceiling and there was a mirror on one of the walls. A row of three windows, high up the wall, were thick and had frosted-glass in them. Couldn't see out. Couldn't see in.

Feeling very sore, Jack sat down and waited. Seemed ages before anyone came in, but eventually two people did. A man and a woman. Also in plain clothes.

The man pulled up a chair and turned it round, resting his arms over the back. The woman just sat down facing Jack. The guy introduced himself and his colleague as Detectives Sergeant Miller and Constable Charnwood. Jack smiled and nodded his head. Hi.

DS Miller switched on the tape machine and began to interview Jack.

"You've had to be brought here, Mr Mason," DS Miller began, "because we believe your life is in danger."

Jack looked gone out. *A bit late to tell me now*, he wanted to tell them.

"Could you tell us in your own words what you did from the time you left work yesterday to being brought here this morning?"

And as Jack began to tell them, the young DC Charnwood started to make notes. Jack thought that was a bit silly since they were recording the conversation.

They wanted to look at his bruises. He just nodded. Saw some of his other scars as well. Looked quite shocked. *Probably seen worse*, he thought.

"You're not under arrest, Mr Mason, so please relax if you can."

Jack found that reassuring and continued with his tale. And when he'd finished DC Charnwood put her note pad down.

"That woman," she asked, flipping back a few pages in her pad, "er Michelle, did you know her very well?"

Jack told her how they'd met whilst jogging along the canal. Didn't tell her Michelle's real name. DC Charnwood pulled a face. "Jogging eh?"

And she began to write again.

"And did this woman come on to you?" she asked.

Jack didn't get chance to reply because the door opened. A man and woman entered the room. It was about three in the afternoon.

"Thank you, DC Charnwood, we'll take it from here."

The two detectives stood up and Jack's face brightened up enough to have lit the entire town.

"Bloody hell."

"Hello Jack," said Major Shaw. "Nice to see you again."

He'd brought some sandwiches and coffee in and, as the two detectives left the room, the food and drink were placed on the table for Jack. He felt tired and just wanted to go to bed, but that wasn't going to be.

"Putting you under police protection, Jack. Going to have to move you to a sort of safe-house for a while, for your own good."

He was now totally confused.

"Let us have your house keys and your phone numbers then we can have someone bring more of your things to you once you're settled in."

Jack handed Geoff his house keys and car keys and told him his phone numbers, and the burglar alarm code.

"Has anyone got a key to your house though?"

"So far as I know only Helen."

They looked at each other and nodded.

Eventually, Jack was asked to sign his statement, sign for the release of his keys, and check that the statement was correct. Then, he was led out to the back of the station by another officer, but before he went any further, Jack was asked to put a hood over his head. Almost a bit of déjà vu. Then he was led to a car. Jack was going to get in the front seat but his escort opened the rear door and told him to get in. He heard someone catch some keys and the driver got in.

It was dark by then and as they drove away Jack had no idea where he was going. It wasn't a long journey and Jack thought they'd ended up somewhere on the outskirts of Stafford, but he wasn't sure. Once again no one spoke a word.

Eventually the car drew up and stopped. Jack was told to remove the hood which he willingly did and after screwing his eyes up a few times he saw they were in a dark narrow street. Then he saw his driver.

"Can't get away from me that easily mate," he joked.

Greg clasped his hand.

"Happier now, Jack?"

They hugged each other like old buddies do and Jack then

followed Greg as he walked quickly along the street and into an alley that led to the back of a row of large, old terraced houses. They went through a tall iron gate and along what looked like a short, narrow garden. At the back door of the house Greg paused, then, as if by magic, it opened. And inside an old hallway they were met by another guy who said hello. Jack watched as the door closed behind them.

"I'm Harry," the man said, holding out his hand.

Jack shook it.

"And I'm Jack."

Harry didn't say anything to Greg though. Just automatically accepted him.

109

"What d'you mean he wasn't there?" Declan snapped.

Rachel shook her head.

"I'll have to speak to Pat and let him know," he growled. "And he'll not be very pleased about it either, mark my words."

Rachel was tired out. The journey had taken a lot longer than she'd expected and the snow hadn't helped.

"You sure you looked, woman?" Declan barked again.

She could almost feel his words hitting her face.

She was getting fed up with Declan's questions.

"Couldn't even see any footprints," she sighed. "It was a bloody white-out up there. Snow must have covered everything."

Declan shook his head and sighed deeply.

"Stupid fuckin' wankers!" he shouted.

"Don't blame the guys who picked him up from his house, Dec," she said. "It was the driver's fault for not giving him a bit of lead poisoning."

Declan shook his head slowly.

"Nah," he sneered. "It was all of them. The two who didn't hog-tie him properly and the driver for just dumping him up there."

110

"Well Jack," Harry said before beginning his lecture on the safe house. "In the day-time this place looks like an old book shop from the front and sometimes we do actually get people come in to buy books, but it's very rare."

Greg winked at him.

He opened the door into the 'shop'.

It looked like something out of a Charles Dickens novel. There was a large window that was filthy with cobwebs, dust, and dead flies. He read the sign on the window through the thin blind that was pulled down to the low windowsill. Moses' Book Shop it said. Jack reckoned it might have been the same age.

He kept looking round expecting to see Scrooge. Everything was brown and looked like it hadn't been painted since it had been built.

There were thousands of books though which made it look interesting. Shelves and shelves of them filled the wall spaces and there were more on tables and some more piled up under them on the floor. But they were all covered in dust and cobwebs. There was a counter with a till at one end as if it were still doing business. Harry had told him because they did get the odd one or two customers, everything had to look correct. And it did.

Jack and Greg were led up a flight of stairs that had one light hanging from the ceiling. Just a bare bulb. Probably a forty watt from the light it gave off. No carpets. Just floorboards. And at the top of the stairs were three doors to other rooms, but Jack was told two of them were always locked. His was open and Harry explained that it wouldn't close properly. Too much paint on it. Jack raised an eyebrow.

"Oh don't worry, Jack," he said with a humorous smile on his face. "You'll be safe as houses."

Jack wasn't that convinced, but he and Greg followed Harry into the room where Jack was going to live. It was really three rooms that were separated by one of those beaded curtains that you could walk through.

The lounge was small and had the mandatory cobwebs at the window. It was one of those sash types and it opened too. Net curtains hung from it. The others looked old and tatty but at least he could draw them. And the view from the window was the back of a row of more old buildings that should have been pulled down years ago.

In Jack's main room, his so-called lounge, was a sofa. Old and lived in. A two-seater. Looked comfortable. There was a small armchair too and just under the window below the radiator was a square rug made from other pieces of material. Reminded him of his childhood. Had one in front of the hearth. Next to a chair was a table. A small TV and a reading lamp sat on it.

Opposite the window was the small kitchen. A sink with a couple of cupboards either side. Above and below. Had no doors. The ones below had an old curtain hung in their place, fastened on a plastic-covered wire that stretched across the gap. A small two-ring electric cooker and oven was next to it and a kettle waited to be switched on. Sugar, coffee, and tea took up one of the shelves above the sink unit and in the top drawer of the lower cupboard were the knives, forks, and spoons plus other utensils that might be needed.

Through the curtain from this lounge was the bedroom. Same size as the lounge. Similar grimy sash window. Similar cobwebs and dead flies. Similar curtains.

Under the window and next to the radiator was a single bed

whose mattress looked like it would hug you when you got into bed and make you feel like the sausage in a hot-dog. Not comfortable. A small bedside table with a lamp stood next to it. Two drawers but not a Gideon's bible to be seen anywhere. Another small rug lay by the bedside. Then, bare floorboards.

On the other side of the bedroom was another curtain which led into the bathroom. A shower was over the bath. A sink was near the end of it and next to that was the loo. There was a cupboard with a boiler in it and it was on. Jack was happy with that. It was freezing outside, and he'd had enough of the cold weather for a while.

Harry took them both downstairs and led them to another room at the back of the so-called shop. It was full of electronic gear.

"This is the ops room," Harry explained, "that's how I knew you were coming, but we've not had to use it for a while."

Jack could see the gadgets, the computers, the printers, other electronic devices, and the TV monitors. One of the cameras clearly covered the path up the garden to the back door. Another let Harry see the front, and two more were set high up in the roof somewhere, giving him a three-hundred-and-sixty-degree view.

They went into the shop where Jack browsed through some of the book titles. There was a pretty good selection too, once the dust was brushed off them. He picked one up.

"You can still go out if you want," Harry told him. "But it would be better if you didn't go out in the daytime."

He winked.

Jack wondered if Harry thought he was a bloody vampire or something and it made him chuckle.

"Am I allowed to contact anyone, Harry?" he asked.

"As well as Greg, a friend of yours has already been vetted and given the all clear so you can call or meet her, but she has been warned not to say anything about where you are. Or why. And you can't have visitors here."

"So where could I meet them then?"

"You mean Steph, don't you?"

Jack nodded, wondering how the hell they knew it was her.

Greg smiled.

"Just down the road there's a pub," he told Jack. "Not a bad place either. It's called The Bowling Alley. The local plods use it so it's quite a safe place to drink."

"So that's where I am. Know it well, Greg," he said, "And thanks Harry, but I reckon some sleep is what I need right now so if you don't mind, I think I'll go upstairs."

Jack was yawning his head off.

"Just one more thing before you go," Harry added. "There's a security number to get in through the back door."

And he wrote it down for him.

"The front door is open from nine to six, like a shop would be, but try not to use it if possible."

Jack nodded, looked at the security number, gave the piece of paper back to Harry, and before trudging up the stairs he told Greg he'd call him later.

Once upstairs Jack made himself a coffee and got undressed. He sent a text to Steph to tell her he wouldn't be at work for some time and to make an excuse to the boss. He was sure Roger wouldn't mind if he knew what had happened.

111

Rachel was on the phone when Declan came in.

"You're always on the bloody phone, woman! It's a wonder the entire world's secret bloody services haven't been listening to you."

She blinked at him then smiled. And delving into her handbag she took out a keyring with two keys on it. She held it up high, letting the keys dangle just of front of Declan's face.

He looked quite amazed.

"Clever girl," he said slowly. "Very clever. Much trouble was it?"

"Piece o'piss," she giggled.

"How d'you manage it then, you said you weren't there very long?"

Rachel gave him one of her crafty smiles.

"Took it off one of the hooks in the hallway and got it pressed when I went to the loo."

She smiled to herself as she remembered when she'd kissed Jack, how, whilst he was enjoying her lips on his, she'd lifted the keys off the hook.

Declan shook his head in disbelief.

"Crafty bugger. What else d'you get?" he asked as if he wasn't satisfied with what she'd done.

She stroked her chin with a finger and thumb, thinking *wouldn't you like to know?*

"There was nothing we'd want," she came back eventually. "What were you hoping for, Dec?"

He looked totally fed up and shrugged his shoulders.

"Don't know, babe," he said. "Just thought there might have been things that could have been fuckin' valuable, that was all."

She studied him.

"With the keys in our pockets we can take a look round ourselves anytime, can't we?" she suggested.

"Mmm, suppose so, but remember we don't know where the fuck he is right now, do we? So we'd have to very careful."

Rachel laughed.

"Careful's my first name, remember."

112

Steph returned Jack's call the next day from work, to tell him that the police had been to see Mr Adams. Thought it might have been to do with him. She wanted to know if she could meet him somewhere, so he told her to be at The Bowling Alley.

"What, Lichfield?" she asked. "Thought you'd be fuckin' miles away."

"I'm going to try and get my laptop here, Steph, then I can still do the accounts from here instead of the office. I'll ring Roger later and explain. Reckon he'll understand especially if the police's visit was to do with me eh?"

She chuckled and wished him luck.

"What time tonight though?"

"Shall we say seven?" Jack asked. "I'll lurk outside and wait for you OK?"

"Lurking is it? No bloody wonder they've put you away." She laughed. "At the back?"

"Yeah, by that door to the bowling-green."

She laughed again.

There was a short pause then she said, "Oh, I forgot to tell you, Rob knows about you being kidnapped. Told him yesterday. Sends his regards."

Jack said thanks and asked her to tell him to be careful too and when he finished the call there was a knock on his door. Harry.

"Someone downstairs to see you, Jack."

They went downstairs to the back room. DS Miller was there.

"Morning," he grunted. "Just come to tell you your boss's been told and he's sent you your laptop so you can still work and communicate with him if you need to. OK?"

Jack was pleased.

The DS asked him if he was OK there and he told him he was. Thank you.

"Can I ask you something though?" Jack asked.

The DS looked up from his chair.

"Go on."

"How come you picked me up so bloody fast?"

A wry grin spread over the DS's face.

"Well, your Welsh friend, Bryn, thought you were up to no good," he began, "and having got your phone number he rang the local police station and told them about you. They contacted us and here you are."

Jack was quite surprised how quickly the police had responded and wondered then if it might have been Bryn who years ago had passed on information that led to Jack being caught and roughed up a bit by the Para's, his so-called enemy.

DS Miller drank his coffee and stood up.

"We'll be in touch," he said to Jack as he left the room and he nodded an OK. He heard the DS leave through the back door and looked at Harry.

"How far from the pub am I then?"

"Y'sound desperate, Jack."

"I am. Haven't had a pint for a while."

"Good," he said. "Don't want you coming back pissed eh?"

Jack knew what he meant, even though he knew he wouldn't.

He took the laptop back upstairs.

There was wi-fi in the place as well, so he could send e-mails.

Steph would be in her element, but Jack had to warn her that everything they said and did would be monitored.

Jack got the computer set up and sent her an e-mail to make sure everything worked.

'This'll be better than having to text you Jack xx', came her reply.

She was right too, because no one in the office would now see her using her mobile so much.

'Don't misuse it though Steph.'

'As if.'

113

"Well, at least your accounts manager's in a safe place now, Roger," said Doug, sitting in one of the armchairs in the golf club's members' lounge.

"Hmm but the girls in his office keep asking where he's gone," Roger answered.

Doug thought for a minute then smiled.

"Why don't you tell them he's had to go away to look after his sick mother and you've made him take his holidays."

Roger sat back and looked at Doug.

"D'you think they'd buy that? I mean, they're not stupid y'know."

Doug smiled then sipped his brandy.

"If you keep telling them, Roger, they'll believe you, trust me."

Roger lifted his brandy to his lips and drank some.

"So are you in touch with him?" he asked Doug. "I know he still does his work for me, but it must be very worrying for him to be living in that place."

"Oh," replied Doug, with a huge smile on his face, "he's not in prison y'know. Might not be home, but he'll be much safer there."

Roger nodded slightly.

"Don't know much of what goes on in those places, Doug," he admitted. "Well, only what I read in books."

Doug guffawed for a few moments.

"And sometimes, Roger, what you read in your books is absolutely correct. Down to the smallest detail."

They drank their brandy.

"Another one then?" Doug asked.

*

Greg visited Jack several times, keeping him up to date with what was happening at the old mill.

"So are they going to just sit and watch then?"

Greg laughed.

"And listen, mate. Just like we used to in the Balkans."

"Shouldn't think there's much cover though is there?"

"Wasn't where we were either, y'stupid bugger. We've got drones now, Jack, not the big things just a few small ones."

Jack sighed.

"Not up to date, am I?"

"Don't worry mate, you'll catch up when you're out of here."

"And when's that?"

114

Steph knew where the pub was. She parked her car next to some others in its large car park. She knew it was a decent place too. Been there a few times with Rob and the kids, when they'd been out for the day in Lichfield.

She'd already seen Jack lurking outside when she'd driven round the pub that was situated in the centre of what could only be described as a huge roundabout. He hadn't seen her though. She'd got a different car.

Jack was standing near a brick wall, next to the entrance to the actual bowling green. It was a public car park, but if you were a client of the pub you didn't have to pay. Just had to log your car reg into one of the machines inside the pub.

She sneaked up and tapped Jack on his shoulder.

He immediately spun round and crouched low, his hands just in front of him as if about to attack her. Frightened her to death.

"Bloody hell Jack," she shouted at him. "What's got into you?"

He relaxed when he realised it was Steph, but he'd frightened her. Hadn't seen him react like that before. And for a long minute they stood there looking at each other, then Steph moved and kissed him. People going into the pub might have thought they'd been married a long time. It was that sort of a kiss.

Inside the pub though, Jack remembered all the pints he'd drunk there. It was one very large room with smaller areas off it and as you walked in through the double doors the bar stretched in front of you and round to the right.

Jack picked a corner and pointed it out for Steph to go and sit whilst he got her a drink. He'd told her it was the safest place. Could see everyone who came in or went out. Told her it might be full of coppers so she'd have to console herself with just the one small white wine. Just the one. And it'd have to last all night.

When Jack sat down Steph raised her glass.

"Here's to breaking out then," she said and laughed.

"'S not funny, Steph. Have to sleep on my own now," he moaned.

She looked at him, frowning.

"Good!"

She said it so loud that a few people nearby looked across at them. Jack felt embarrassed. He looked around the place. Didn't recognise anyone, but several guys at the bar were looking at them as if they were strangers and hadn't the right to be there. Strange why people do that in pubs.

"So how's the office then?" he asked.

"Typical bloody bloke," she said. "What about me?"

"That's what I meant, girl."

"Wasn't what y'fuckin' said though was it?"

"Stop bloody moaning," he tried to say quietly.

Steph placed one hand over his and smiled.

"Rob's been helping the plods."

Jack leaned forward, closer to her, listening to what she was going to say next.

"He got the reg numbers of the two vehicles he saw the other night. Reckon your driver'll be picked up soon."

Jack smiled.

"What's Roger said then?"

Steph shook her head.

"Nothing Jack. Not a bloody thing."

Sipping some of his pint he watched an elderly couple shuffle in. The old guy leant on his stick as he went to the bar whilst his elderly wife eventually took a seat across the room, facing Jack and Steph. He nudged her, nodding his head towards the couple. Steph glanced at them.

"What?" she asked quietly.

"D'you reckon they've just come off duty then?"

Steph chuckled and sipped some wine.

"You're rotten sometimes, Jack Mason. Probably under-cover," she joked.

Jack guffawed, spilling some of his pint and Steph took a tissue from her handbag and wiped his mouth. Just like his Mum used to do. She sat back and smiled proudly at him, now that she'd cleaned him up a bit.

"Won't be able to come out for a couple of nights now, Jack," she told him. "Rob's away and I haven't got a babysitter."

He understood and, reaching across the table, he squeezed her hand.

Eventually, after chatting about nothing in particular, they got up and left the pub, she driving off towards Rugeley and he sauntering along the Friary heading back to the safe-house.

115

"Pat's planning Brendan's escape."

Rachel was shocked.

"And how's he going to do that then?"

"Well, Brendan's been up to his tricks again and has to go to court next week for supposedly beating up his cell-mate."

Rachel frowned.

"A bit dodgy though, isn't it?" she replied. "With all that security?"

Declan nodded.

"He'll do whatever's necessary though and then he and Pat'll get out of sight."

"Where?"

"That old mill I was telling you about. Know it?"

He waited for her reply.

"Know it? Christ my dad used to go to college there. Nelson Hall it was then."

"Yeah, but you didn't know what was under that field though did you?"

"Not then," she told him. "Dad used to say it scared him to bits when he and his friends heard that noise on the way back from the pub at Millmeece."

*

"So that was Steph then?"

Tom nodded.

"Her husband's helping the local guys with the transport thing. Gave some info to them and they're moving faster now. Already picked up the driver and he's being replaced by none other than her husband. Forensics had a field day with Jack's clothes that he had on in the van too. Found traces of C4 on them. Plus some drugs and a bit of gun-oil. And because of the other stuff Rachel's partner's been nicking, they're having a ball. Greg's keeping his eyes on Jack as well. Reckon he's going to be given his old job too from what I've heard."

"He'll have to be careful though," Helen said. "Steph's hubby's a big bloke and if he found out they'd been kissing like they were just before we came in, he'd bloody murder him."

Tom chuckled and raised his pint to his mouth, winking at his elderly friend Helen as she sipped her sherry.

"Good job I like the bloody stuff, Tom," she whispered after finishing it.

"Want another then, old girl?" he joked.

"Watch it mate!" she replied, sounding even more like the elderly lady she was supposed to be.

116

"Dec what's up man?" Rachel asked.

"Cops pulled our driver in the other day. Don't know why. They're holding him for some reason and our legal guy's going to see him in the morning."

"Shit!" she shouted. "It's not to do with what we're doing, is it?"

She looked quite pale and worried.

"Don't think so," he told her. "His bird said it was about a bloke he nearly killed some years back. Found some DNA. That's why they're holding him."

Rachel let out a long deep sigh.

"Phew. Thank God for that."

She hurriedly drank some more of her wine.

"So who's on the job now then?"

"Oh, one of Roger's other drivers. New guy. Huge bloke too. Thick as shit though."

"Aren't they all?" she laughed.

"Yeah, but they do as they're told so don't knock 'em OK?"

"Can you trust this one though?"

Declan nodded very slowly.

"He's already been told what he has to do and like the dumb-shit he is, he's accepted the money too."

Rachel smiled but wasn't too sure.

"So how d'you know he'll keep his mouth shut then?"

Declan's face took on a vicious look.

"There's a wife and three kids at home."

117

"I was in The Bridge the other night, Jack, and Paul's partner was there with another bloke. Heard them talking about one of Mr Adams' drivers. Cops have evidently picked him up, but two weeks before, Rob was asked by the police if he'd like to start driving for Mr Adams. He's agreed as well. They told him he looks the part, whatever they meant by that."

Jack listened.

"Tell him to act fucking dumb then, Steph."

"That's just what the police told him to do. Well not the police exactly."

"Who was it then, Steph?"

"Some other guys he was chatting to at the station."

"Eh?" Jack gasped. "Others? Who the hell were they then?"

A second or two passed before she spoke again.

"Rob said he didn't know, but he's been told to keep quiet."

Jack wondered if Greg and his friends had something to do with it, then Steph continued.

"He's also been shooting guns as well. Training, he told me."

"What?" queried Jack.

"He said he's OK about it. Seems to be enjoying it too. Told me he knew what to do. Just needed a bit of practice first."

"Practice? How d'you mean, Steph?"

"Oh, didn't I tell you, Jack?" she said, "He was in the army years ago."

She heard Jack's gulp over the phone.

"What was he?" he asked slowly, suspiciously.

"Staff Sergeant, 2 Para."

118

"Declan?"

"What is it?" he snarled angrily at being woken up by the voice on the end of the phone. "It's two o'clock in the fuckin' morning!"

"Sorry mate, but Pat and me just completed the recce. Everything is looking great. There's no one around at night. Don't go in until eight in the morning, so if we choose a night when there's no bloody moon it should only take about an hour to get set up. Then we can blow that Blakemoor woman up when it suits us eh?"

Declan smiled.

"What about cameras?"

Connor laughed.

"Only got them above the doors outside."

"Have we got enough explosives though?"

"Got all we'll need, Dec, but we'll put a bit more with it just to make sure."

"So when are you going to put it in place then?"

"Looking at the calendar it'll have to be next month now. Talk to you about it at the mill later."

119

"Has he got a tattoo of Pegasus down his left side under his arm?"

Steph mumbled a yes, wondering what was coming next.

"How d'you know that?"

"Reckon we've worked together, Steph."

"Eh, where?"

"Balkans," he told her.

"What? He never went there," she told him.

Jack chuckled.

"Believe me, Steph, he did, but he probably wasn't allowed to say anything about it."

She gasped.

"Is that when you got all those nasty scars on your back then?"

Jack swallowed hard.

"No Steph, that was later," he said, eager to forget. "Rob and a couple of his mates managed to get us out of Mostar and back to the relative safety of Sarajevo."

He heard her whistle through her teeth as she tried to take it all in, wondering where he was talking about.

"Went to see them all once I was back in the UK. Found him in the gym at Tidworth."

"I don't fuckin' believe this, Jack," she shouted down the phone. "Does he know?"

"Don't think so, Steph, but don't tell him please. Well not until all this is over, eh?"

"God no, Jack! Suppose I'll have to be careful too now then eh?"

"Yes, you will, especially with the kids, but I'm sure Rob'll tell you what to do. If he doesn't, I'll introduce you to a friend who will."

"Rob's been instructing us every day, Jack," she laughed. "Still thinks he's the Sergeant-bloody Major."

She chuckled.

"But *I* am."

120

Tom and Helen's colleagues had been through as much as they could with Rob. Greg was happy with his weapon-handling skills even though they were a bit rusty and much to Rob's delight he was now firing the very country's latest weapons. Wished he'd had them years ago.

He'd also been given some small tracking devices that could be attached to anyone or anything. Just in case. Made Rob feel very much at home. He wanted to blow the suspects to kingdom come, but Greg's friends only frowned at him after he'd suggested how. And they all hoped he wouldn't.

The change-over of drivers was carried out as if it were normal, just like it was whenever Mr Adams wanted a new driver.

And before Rob took the driver's job with Roger's Transport, the advert went in the local paper.

*

"... escaped from the vehicle that was taking the prisoner to Birmingham Crown Court," the newsreader explained to the TV viewers and a photo of Brendan came up on the screen. "The police said he is dangerous, might be armed, and that he must not be approached. And if anyone sees him, they are to ring this number."

A phone number then flashed up on the TV screen for a few seconds.

Brendan, Rachel, Declan, Connor, Pat, and Michael laughed, chinking their glasses together.

"Well done Pat lad," Brendan told him after watching the news headlines in the office. He switched the TV off. "So, this'll be my home for a while then, will it?"

"Until June, after the job's done, Brendan."

He looked at them.

"Then things'll really go mad, eh?"

He looked at Pat.

"The explosives are being put in place next month. And then, when lady bloody Blakemoor opens the new exhibition hall ... BOOOOM and the lot of them will be gone for good."

Brendan grinned.

"Am I involved?"

"You weren't supposed to be, but since you're out I dare say your expertise will be gratefully accepted."

They raised their glasses and drank the whisky down in one.

121

"We understand the job's in June," Sir David was telling the team. "It will be called Fly By Night."

He paused for effect.

"A couple of our guys will be with some of the armed response unit of the Staffordshire force when they pick up the drivers from Roger's transport and hold them for questioning. There'll be a total news blackout."

"Cassie, Helen, and Tom, your role though will be to pick up these terrorists just as they think they're detonating the bombs."

Heads turned to face each other again. "Greg and Jack, you, along with some officers from the Staffordshire ARU will be responsible for bringing in those left at the mill, however, we understand that the woman Rachel, as she's now called, will probably be still working in Stafford, so be prepared to move fast, gentlemen."

"As from today some of our friends from twenty-two Regiment will be watching and waiting. Their role is to find the explosive devices and remove them after they've been planted. They'll be deep undercover, keeping eyes on because we believe one or two of the suspects will on the day have to be near enough to press the button for the signal to fire the detonators. And that's when nothing will go bang. They won't be too far away, so when nothing happens they'll be confused and you'll be able to hold them for the police to make the arrests."

Sir David paused when Major Shaw handed him a note. He read it, smiled, winking and nodding to his colleague.

"The opening of the RAF Museum's new exhibition hall at Cosford will go ahead as planned, but only if the explosives have been found and taken away. And when Cassie and her team pick up their targets, the other members will be picked up at the mill.

"You'll all be armed. And should anything go wrong, everything will be hastily cancelled. You won't be involved with that."

There was a pause for the laughter to subside.

"But nothing will go wrong though, will it?"

And looking more serious they watched the boss point to various places on the large map of the museum and its surrounding area.

"Naturally the security will be very high considering who's cutting the ribbon. You all know how much she and I don't get on, so let's be even more professional than we may want to be."

He paused.

"Mrs Blakemoor will be doing it. Her bloody entourage will be with her too. Just hope she doesn't get talking about the detente she's hoping to have with the Irish."

Heads turned, wondering what he was talking about. Some muttered quietly among themselves. Only a few were in the know.

"So, ladies and gentlemen, that's the plan."

They all gathered round the map, studying it again, before paying more attention to the 6ft square model that covered two large tables.

"Study it and remember as much of it as you can. Don't be afraid to ask questions if you're not sure. You will all be making a visit, taking a look for yourselves of course, but separately, and as paying visitors."

They all laughed. Thought the paying bit was a joke. Then they realised it wasn't. They moved around the table.

"We'll go through the security arrangements tomorrow, OK?"

And leaving the room Sir David picked up his phone.

122

Brendan looked at his watch.

"Time to go, lads," he said, then he looked at Rachel. "Sorry girl, you'll have to stay here with Pat and keep watch on Michael. He's getting jittery."

She laughed. She wasn't pleased but she understood. Brendan didn't like women being on the firing line in case they were caught and his guys tried to save her. Could lose them all that way.

Brendan, Sean, Declan, and Connor loaded their vehicles with the haversacks full of explosives. Two people in each car. Rachel, Pat, and Michael waved them off from the mill and went back inside, sliding the large metal door closed.

Because of the amount of explosives they had to carry, they had to go to Cosford two nights on the trot. They'd look like a couple of RAF lads going back to camp.

As the cars drove away, their occupants were completely unaware that eyes in the sky were following their every move. Keeping unseen people updated on the route they were taking.

Driving to Newport, then down the A41 they dropped Declan and Connor off not far from the museum. Brendan and Sean then turned around and drove back a few miles, to the other side of the M54 and parked up in a quiet road just off the A41. Once Declan and Connor had planted their bombs they cut across the fields to the A41 to meet their friends and get back to the mill.

123

A few miles south of the city of Lincoln was once one of the homes to one of the UK's V-Bomber forces. Now, long after the Valiants, the Victors, and the Vulcans had been retired from service, it had become home to much more modern aircraft. And some of these had no pilot on board.

Word came down from people at the top to have one of them fly high above the West Midlands. Circling round, unseen and out of the way of all civilian aircraft, it was to be an exercise for the newly trained crews who flew these aircraft from their porta-cabins on the ground, guarded within the highly secret area of this RAF station.

For these pilots it came as a brief and enjoyable change from focussing on the ground over Afghanistan and its neighbours, wiping out in seconds those sub-human lives whose sole intentions were to kill, maim, and destroy everything.

The pilots joked perhaps there were a few other undesirables in the area over which they were now guiding these un-manned aircraft.

124

Watching Declan and Connor move to their targets to plant the explosives, the guys from 22 Regiment were smiling to themselves. They only wished they could take them out there and then, but they couldn't. They hoped if anything went tits up and shots were fired there was every possibility of them being killed, but the two men were to be taken alive.

Several guys from this elite group of men were already inside the buildings, hidden inside some of the aircraft on display, whilst others on the roofs were peering through the cracks that had been specially made. And with their micro-cameras they were able to see exactly where Declan and Connor planted their devices. Once they were seen leaving the buildings a bleep on their coms to their friends outside alerted them to keep eyes on and make sure they were well away from the area before their colleagues could undo all their work.

By 2.15 a.m. Declan and Connor were at Sean and Brendan's cars.

"All done," Connor said as they drove away, heading back to the mill.

"Told you there wasn't anyone around, didn't I?"

Brendan laughed.

"Won't be like that soon though, will it?"

"We'll have to really be careful then cos the whole place'll be surrounded by security people of one form or another."

As they drove along the A41 to Newport, in the light of the early morning's dawn, none of them had any idea that they'd been seen by at least twenty people. And that didn't include those at RAF

Waddington either. They'd just spent their shifts transmitting pictures from above the West Midlands.

Cassie and Helen found them on their tracker. They were just going through the small town of Eccleshall and would be back at the mill in less than ten minutes.

"They won't be long," Cassie told Greg, who was with some of their friends watching the mill.

"Thanks Cass. But there's only one person here at the moment."

125

For the rest of the month everyone was becoming tense. Those watching had nothing to report. Those being watched were in the mill whilst Declan and Rachel were back at Declan's home in Rugeley, under the eyes of Greg and Jack.

In London the Prime Minister was being given her instructions. What she had to do, who she was going to meet and where. She moaned about not being allowed to invite to her opposite number in Dublin. Somewhat annoyed she went back to Downing Street with a sour look on her face, cursing all the way in the back of her chauffeured car. And after dropping her off, her security team laughed all the way back to their office.

Steph's husband had also been told to stand by, just in case, but from that he thought it sounded like he wouldn't be required. And whilst being thankful for that, he did feel a bit peed off about it. After all, having been in the Paras, Rob was now wanting a bit of the action.

*

"What's up Rachel?"

She threw her handbag down on the settee.

"Remember the driver they picked up? His partner was talking to one of his mates. Told her that guy had been in the Paras."

Declan's head swivelled round fast.

"Y'what?"

"Said that the new driver at Roger's Transport had been seen chatting to the cops as well. And worse still, he reckoned he was going to be involved with some sort of sting to do with the missing wine."

Declan drew in a deep breath then slowly released it.

"What's your babysitting skills like then, love?"

Rachel sniggered at first and realised what he meant. She swallowed hard.

"You want me to kinap the family then?"

"No. Just pay them a visit. Keep your gun on them during the time the job takes. I'll text you, then leave. Fast!"

"But what if Roger doesn't use her old man?"

"I'll let you know beforehand, babe. Don't worry about it, OK?"

126

By the time of the opening of the RAF Museum's new exhibition hall, almost one hundred and fifty pounds of C4 explosives had been safely removed and the whole place had been secured and made safe. Sniffer dogs had been all over the grounds. All the sewers along the nearby roads had been checked and their entrances sealed off, as were the metal lids on every drain cover.

On the day sniffer dogs were everywhere. Everyone was frisked, their bags searched like they would be at an airport and that was only one of several security procedures that the public was met with. Ticket holders were directed to their various stands to watch the ceremony. VIPs, and there were many, were escorted to the large reception area, specially built to accommodate them so they could meet, greet, and have drinks before the ceremony began. Inside it a band from the RAF was providing musical entertainment to those privileged to be in The Lounge, as it was called. They'd be there for most of the afternoon too, having luncheon when the official opening ceremony had finished and the public were allowed to view the new hall for themselves.

Armed police wandered around the grounds whilst under-cover people mingled with the crowds that were pouring in. By ten-thirty in the morning, everyone was fully aware that the Prime Minister was about to arrive.

Coming along the road from RAF Cosford for everyone to see, three police motorcyclists provided the escort for the Prime Minister and her entourages' cars making their way to the where a guard of honour from the Queen's Colour Squadron of the Royal Air Force was lined up. Behind them, the Royal Air Force's Central Band had taken post, waiting to play their part in the ceremony.

All eyes were on the Prime Minister as she left the car. It was only then, when the other VIPs had taken their places facing the parade, that Mrs Daphne Blakemoor took her place on the dais. Everyone there stood up. The Guard Commander shouted out his orders for the general salute and the band began playing the National Anthem. Only the first six bars though. She wasn't the Queen.

Mrs Blakemoor inspected the guard and then returned to the saluting dais. A few words from the guard commander and the guard marched off, followed by the band playing *Those Magnificent Men In Their Flying Machines.*

127

Hidden deep among the bushes and hedgerows almost half a mile away, two men were watching the ceremony and when the Prime Minister cut the ribbon in front of the new hall, one of them pressed his thumb hard onto the red button.

The fingers of the security service's teams tightened across the triggers of their weapons. And the fingers of some were already on them.

Suddenly there was a huge cheer when the ribbon fell to the ground, cut in two by the scissors the Prime Minister was now handing back to her personal assistant. She smiled briefly at the crowd as she moved away to the new exhibition hall's entrance, escorted by a high-ranking member of the RAF. She waved again to the crowd and disappeared into the hall and the crowd began to move from their seats.

In the hedgerow where Brendan and Declan had been allowed to hide for the last twenty-four hours, confusion reigned. Nothing had happened. There hadn't been an explosion. Declan pressed the button again and again but still nothing was happening. They looked at each other, wondering why. As they looked at each other Declan's face changed. Confusion became fear.

Then Brendan suddenly felt the muzzle of a weapon pushing hard into his head.

128

A loud banging on the door startled Sean. He was at Declan's house and he wasn't expecting visitors. Not that time in the morning. Still dressed, he got up and snatched his Beretta 92F from under the pillow. Along the landing he snapped in the fifteen-round magazine. One hollow-tipped round went straight in the chamber. Made pancake-sized holes. He checked the safety. Down. Off.

Sean was at the top of the stairs when the door burst open, crashing to the floor, followed by five people in black. Full combat gear. One behind the other. Weapons raised. Ready to fire.

They split up and ran into each room downstairs. All clear. But Sean was still on the landing. One of the intruders nodded towards the stairs. Covered by his friends, he was just about to put one foot on the first step when there was a loud bang. He went down. Winged in the leg by a round from the Beretta. He'd be off work for a while. One of the men dragged him away. Left him outside for his colleagues to take him to the medics that were nearby with officers from the local police force.

The man came back in and mumbled to the others. They knew what the weapon was. Sean wondered if he could get out from one of the upstairs windows and darted into his bedroom. He heard the noise of people running up the stairs.

It was just about light when he stood on the flat roof at the back of Declan's house. There was a noise. He pointed the Beretta in the direction of it. Pulled the trigger. Heard a shout as if the round had hit someone. Heard another noise behind him. A shot rang out, followed quickly by a second one. Double tap. From Sean's head a thin pink cloud filled the space around him. And Sean's body slumped to the floor.

129

At the mill, after the explosives had been planted, Connor had left. Hadn't been missed. He'd walked away from the mill in the middle of the night with two RPG's and some explosives plus detonators in his haversack. He was on a mission of his own.

He'd realised there would be far too much security around the museum. He'd argued about it with Brendan and Sean, but he hadn't convinced them. So, after the argument, he told them it wasn't a good plan. Said he was moving elsewhere and hoped to join them if their plan were successful.

He reached his car that he'd left in a lane near a farmhouse a couple of miles away in Standon and drove off to a friend's home to wait a few days until it was all over. His friend was away on holiday, so Connor had the place to himself.

In the house he had all he wanted. There was plenty of food and, to make things better, he'd bought a lot of drink in case he could celebrate Mrs Blakemoor's demise.

He watched TV. He listened to the radio, but nothing was mentioned about a bombing at the RAF Museum. It would've been headline news. There was, however, just a few minutes, showing the Prime Minister cutting the ribbon and opening the hall. Something had gone wrong.

That made Connor very angry and he began to drink heavily.

130

Declan had put up quite a fight, but he was no match for Cassie, Helen, and Tom. They were over him like flies on a piece of shit. Smashing their fists into his face, into his body, and kicking every part of him that would cause pain. Declan was eventually knocked out. Brendan was already cuffed with plastic ties and now so too was his friend. Having broken his nose, several fingers, and a few ribs in the struggle, Declan was beaten. Cassie's lips were swollen, Tom was nursing his grazed chin, and Helen was only slightly bruised, happy in the knowledge that she'd done most of the rib cracking.

Brendan and his friend were then handed over to four SAS guys who were nearby. Unceremoniously they grabbed the two men and, after giving them a few more kicks, they flung them both head first into the back of a van like sacks of coal, to be taken to the police who were waiting nearby to arrest them, before being handed over to MI6 for interrogation.

Info passed over the radios between the teams. Sir David smiled as Mrs Blakemoor was later told of the operation. She immediately wanted to hold a press conference to tell the world how good *her* security forces had once again been. Wanted to stand there in front of the world's TV looking as if she had put the plan together. As if she had done all the fighting. She held her head high. Proud.

Until Sir David told her the terrorists were from Dublin.

She stamped her foot down hard on the floor of his office in Vauxhall. Had to wait until the operation was finally over. Had to wait and listen to the info that was coming into the office. Seething within whilst trying to smile at the men and women who were by Sir David's side.

131

The police officers at the mill rushed in and arrested Michael. Thought there'd be more people there. Twenty to one. He didn't have a chance. They took him away to a secure cell.

Sean had been shot. There wasn't much to see. Only two holes. Two neat holes. Just above his eyebrows, closely grouped. But the back of his head was a different kettle of fish. Or brains.

In a black bag, after the photos had been taken, his body was half-carried, half-dropped on its way to the van that was to take him to the morgue. Another body. Another statistic. But another dead terrorist.

Meanwhile Greg and Jack had split up. Greg was at the supermarket in Stafford where Rachel worked. He was told that she hadn't been to work for two days. He immediately phoned Jack.

"She's elsewhere, Jack. I'll keep looking though."

But Jack's phone only crackled. For some reason it seemed out of range. No one was answering it. Greg was worried. Wondered why. Wondered where Jack was. Ideas were rushing through his mind. And he was beginning to fret.

Fifteen minutes later and he was speaking on the phone to Helen. Asked her if she had any idea where he might be.

"He'll be going for Rachel," she fired back quickly.

It was at that moment that a very ugly scene came straight into his head.

132

Only two people were in the house. Both of them were women. But only one had a gun. And it wasn't Steph. She was tied to a chair with one of the kids' skipping ropes. She could have struggled free, but she didn't. With a gun in her face she thought better of it. She remembered her husband saying 'run away bravely' when she got upset about things. Besides, she was only going to be like this until he had finished his work delivering the wine.

Rachel looked at her watch. She frowned. She was working out how long the job should have taken, and Steph's husband was long overdue.

"So, where's the kids today?" she snarled.

"With their aunty," was Steph's short reply.

"Bit of a coincidence, isn't it?"

She looked at her watch again.

"They go there every week."

Rachel was becoming agitated. Didn't like having to wait. Steph noticed too.

"Expect the police'll be here soon."

Rachel sneered.

"Why them?"

Steph turned to face her as best she could.

"Your little van job will have failed."

"How d'you mean?"

"That's why Rob's late."

Rachel was about to hit Steph in the face, but the sound of

footsteps on the gravel outside stopped her. She looked round and raised her weapon. Her Walther PPK.

Two doors in the kitchen flew open at the same time. Rachel looked at one. The door from the hall. Just saw a very large guy. Didn't need to aim. Her target was too big to miss from there. She was just about to fire when she was distracted. Jack came in through the back door.

"Hello again Briony," he said calmly, quietly.

The sun was behind him and Rachel had to squint. Still pointing her gun at Rob, she half turned to look at Jack. She wondered how he knew her, then realised he must have been part of the team that set her up in London. She glared at him. Then took aim at Rob.

Steph screamed. Jumped when the gun went off. Hadn't heard one before. Not that close. And when the dust settled, she peered through the smoke that drifted across the kitchen. She cried as Rob began to undo the skipping rope with one hand. Tried to hug him. Saw the blood pouring down his arm.

Two shots had been fired. Rob had taken a round in his shoulder. Rachel had shot him. But she'd been facing Jack. Too late to point her weapon at him. And the second shot knocked Rachel over. Killed her. Messy sight for Steph to see. Rob hurried her out into the back garden where he was attended to by medics who were called from the street. She was in shock.

Minutes later she was joined by Jack. She ran to him, hugged him, and kissed him.

"Put me down, woman!" he joked.

Even Rob chuckled.

133

Pat had gone underground, eventually joining up with Connor who was drinking more heavily. They were living in Ashbourne and were chatting about how their plans had gone to pieces.

In the George & Dragon they were sitting in a corner seat having Sunday lunch when one of Connor's old acquaintances slid into the seat next to them. Both Connor and Pat looked at him.

"Got a job you'd like," he told them and from his coat pocket he pulled a large envelope out and dropped it on the table. Looked heavy.

"Go on. Take a look," he whispered, urging them on.

Connor tipped the end of the envelope up and glanced inside.

Pat saw his reaction and raised his eyebrows. He shot Connor a look. His other friend nodded.

"Three thousand," the man whispered.

Then Connor took a piece of paper from the envelope.

Written on it was a map showing details of a journey. There was a time and a date on it too.

Connor showed it to Pat, and they nodded in unison. The other man asked if it was on. They shook hands and the man left them to finish their lunch.

"This'll be easy, Con. The woman's travelling with her old man. Must be up to something dodgy eh?"

"They've even marked the map where the best place to do it is as well."

"And we'll get to use those RPG's after all too."

134

After the celebrations of another successful operation, life went back to being normal again. But in a slightly different way. Rob's mum had passed away just after the museum incident. He and Steph talked about moving. Steph thought it a good idea. A fresh start. Somewhere she'd wanted to live but hadn't been able to because of Rob's Mum's outrageous attitude.

She told Jack they were leaving. Said she'd miss him, and she'd always love him. She never mentioned to Rob that he and Jack had worked together, even though she still had no idea where the Balkans were, but she thought he knew after the way Jack had killed Rachel. Thought he'd seen him do that before somewhere else.

Paul was jailed for a few months and after being released he went to live in Salford.

Tom continued working with six. Looking. Hearing. Watching and listening. So too did Helen. She stayed with Jack sometimes if she was in the area.

And Jack went back to his job as accounts manager with Roger's Transport, albeit still in the pay of the security services.

As for PC Cookson and his adventurous son Josh, nothing was ever mentioned about the pipes he'd found that day with his friend Bill.

135

It was early one morning. The middle of July. Mr and Mrs Blakemoor had been the only ones on the road. They'd been on their way to Buxton. Without the knowledge of the security services, a secret meeting had been arranged with the Irish Prime Minister and his wife. And Mrs Blakemoor had told Sir David she was taking a break for a few days, instructing him that she was *not* to be followed or contacted. She said she'd wanted to get away from everything for a while. The signed memo said so.

At ten o'clock, though, Mrs Blakemoor's face had taken over the news. Her car had been found. Burnt and wrecked beyond belief. One of two cars. Both in pieces along the same road. Police had found the remains of two bodies that had been thrown away from the wreckage. An explosion had occurred. Two other bodies were found in the other car that had crashed into a tree after swerving over the road. Skid marks were being measured. All four bodies were in a local morgue awaiting a post-mortem examination. They presumed the driver of the other car and his passenger had been drinking. Very heavily. Their charred remains stunk of whisky. Police believed Mr and Mrs Blakemoor had been killed by terrorists. Parts of a rocket-propelled grenade launcher had been found in the other wreckage, together with other smaller weapons.

The Queen had been informed. Sent her condolences to Mrs Blakemoor's family and asked that the country's flags be lowered to half-mast. Bittersweet words of respect.

In their prisons, Declan, Michael, and Brendan had heard the news and smiled. Hadn't understood who'd done it, but they'd had a good guess.

Meanwhile, in Sir David's office, just after attending the late PM's funeral, he and Geoff were having a drink. Their own private wake. An empty bottle of Talisker lay on its side, slowly moving around in circles on his desk and a second bottle, now in Sir David's hand, was almost empty. He and the Major were pleasantly merry. And very pleased too. They raised their glasses.

"Here's to our new Prime Minister," Sir David said, slurring his words a little.

Geoff guffawed. Huge belly laughs rang around the office.

"You're a nasty bugger when you want to be, Dave."

Sir David topped up their glasses and smiled at his friend.

"Manage to call in a favour then?" Geoff asked.

Poker-faced, Sir David looked at Geoff.

"Haven't a clue what you're talking about."

ABOUT THE AUTHOR

Chris Breddy served in the Royal Air Force for twenty-six years, after which he went in a different direction which added even more to his life's experiences. He began writing after wondering how certain books he'd read had become best-sellers. Deciding to write one himself, he put pen to paper, and this is his first attempt. He's also currently writing others of a similar genre.

Printed in Great Britain
by Amazon